# Navigating Home

## New Writing from Orkney

First published in 2010 by **The George Mackay Brown Fellowship**
In association with Scottish Arts Council, Orkney Islands Council and Leader

Scottish Arts Council

ORKNEY ISLANDS COUNCIL

LEADER

this project is being part-financed by the
Scottish Government and the European Community
Orkney LEADER 2007-2013 Programme

compiled and edited by **Nalini Paul**
designed by **Iain Ashman**

images by **Christina Sargent**



ISBN 978-0-9566616-0-9

Printed by The Orcadian Ltd, Hell's Half Acre, Hatston, Kirkwall, Orkney, KW15 1DY

# Navigating Home

## New Writing from Orkney

To Alan,

Here's to "home" in all of its time-lit manifestations.

Love,

Nalini xx

Stromness

October, 2010.

gmb

THE GEORGE MACKAY BROWN FELLOWSHIP

# contents

# introduction

The writing in this anthology reflects themes of migration, memory and landscapes, which I have woven into my projects and collaborations over the year as George Mackay Brown Writing Fellow. Art forms used in the Johnsmas Foy, from poetry to music and song, to Orkney Traditional Dance and visual art, addressed questions of place, identity and belonging. Workshops and tours led by World Heritage Site rangers touched on issues of the past, and memory that transcends the written word. Bird watching tours with the RSPB highlighted the fluidity of identities through migration.

The idea of home resonates, because we are all from somewhere else (one way or another), and we often return. But for many I have met, befriended and worked with over the year, home is not necessarily confined to one, fixed place. Home can be where one grew up, but it is not always here. People visit the place of their childhood or birth, and return after living elsewhere. George Mackay Brown himself, ventured sooth only when he felt it was necessary. Despite his sense of rootedness, his writing is never parochial. Rather, it acknowledges the ever-changing nature of all cultures, far from being fixed or static. Like the Orkney folk songs and stories that have travelled from Norway to Orkney to Canada, and beyond – changing en route, to make any sense of the "original" difficult and misleading – so the writing that follows reflects some of the shifts taking place in our cultural landscape.

Above all else, home is a place to feel welcome, and to share a sense of belonging. Like birds that migrate – sometimes thousands of miles each year – we find our home in the places we have visited or lived, where we raise our children, where we were born, or where we decide to live. Orkney is a place that will never leave me, whether I stay, leave, or return again, sometime in the near future.

**Nalini Paul** GMB Writing Fellow 2009-10

# Memory

GUILLEMOTS

## Amber Connolly

# Anwar the Fulmar

Anwar dropped her weight down into the rooty heather of her chosen perch. From here the ancient stone slabs afforded her sufficient cover to watch the Fulmar on the furthest reach of cliff. Each day a change in the glint of his eye.

What would pull him
onward
skyward
a sudden commitment
to release from this place.

Where does that decision
happen
travelling
from bird-brain
to root feet
an impulse
gathering momentum
momentous commitment to launch
ledge-free
into the ever-changing
sky currents.

What would it mean
where
would the balance
of wit and wind
conjure?

Each day Anwar felt the beginnings of another feather pushing its way up from under her skin. Her words were less. Her restlessness grew. Each day a change in the glint of her eye. And the wind pressed into her back.

# Sang the Girl on Rusty Swing

Give me roots
give me wings
sang the girl
on rusty swing.

Sang the girl
on rusty swing
steal not my roots
pray find my wings.

## Lesley Harrison

# Red Head

*cumulus humilis*
a sun-warmed sea; a calm summer morning.
a condensation of light.

*cumulus congestus*
huge, empty castles
toppling over a glittering sea.

*cumulonimbus capillatus*
an updraft emptying the sea.
funnels of wet air.

*stratocumulus perlucidus*
a looming coast, like mountain snow
grey or emerald green.

*altocumulus stratiformis*
intermediate:
a dull quilt of muffled sound.

*nimbostratus*
macular, thickening.
a long grey wave flecked with rubble.

*cirrus spissatus*
a white tent
holding the wind between islands.

## John McGill

# Navigation

Hid wis orange ower Dounby,
But hame at Gerson there's a fine black sky,
a tullimentan sea,
an my heid fair tiftan wi the beer.

*Thoo'll freeze oot there*, says Maggie.

But a man should pee below the sters, an facean Africa.

An buey, the sters are singan!
An Orion's risan, aafil lik a mobile phone,
an Leo like a set o heidphones wi their flex,
An yon gret Northren Cross, yon Swan,
The steeran rods an aixles o a gret John Deere.

I catalogue them in my heid:
The Steeran Rods, the Heidphones an the Mobile Phone -
An high up there abune the hoose,
An dirlan lik a spinnan speeder roon the Pole…

*Hid's aafil lik a Hoover*, Maggie says,
*a ferfil Hoover*, ripan up the sky.

But even gleckit Jock o Millquoy kens the Ploo,
aabody kens the Ploo.

An I think, *we'll mibbe no be ramstam here,*
*we'll mibbe better keep him as he is…*

*we'll keep the Ploo…*

For I think o some puir draigelt pickie-terno,

Birsay-boond, lukkan for the Pointers,
aa in a steer, his wey weel-tyned,
flappan aboot Siberia.

## Museum of Mankind

Qerneg fashioned a needlecase in slow bone
by fitful blubberlight
crouched in her icehouse with Nasuk gone
for walrus. Cunning her hands as night by night
they wrought her love: Nasuk in snow
thumbsized. On show his hunting gear –
quiver and bow,
and taller than he his fourbarbed walrusspear.
Four nights she gave his face
all moonlike in its parkahood and laughed,
cutting his smile, and gave five days
to knowing fingers on a harpoonshaft.

Onatha's plan, her butterflyandbird shoe,
grew three weeks in her head,
till Sesondowah chased the browsing caribou
and freed her hands for thread.
Then nine nights crouched against the dark
she stitched them, beadbright in the wigwam smoke:
the whippoorwill the swallowtail the meadowlark,
bright bobolink and dusky mourning cloak.
She stitched, he stalked, wolfloping by the herd,
and with her last bright bead delivered meat.
She took them up, her twining butterflyandbird,
and laid them shining at the hunter's feet.

Cloakroom Doris, hot behind her hatch,
thanks God and screws her lips.
'Another day,' she says to Bill, and drops the latch.
'Three thousand Yanks and fifty p in tips.
I hate this place at night, I get out quick,
them shrunken heads and things, that funny light,
I don't know why they come, it makes me sick,
them savages. Alf's working late tonight,
just fishandchips. I hope that bloody bus ain't full.'
It is. And so the next, the next. Her dream,
her earlybathandCorrie, fades, and in her skull
Qerneg and Onatha scream.

## Nalini Paul

# Camping

I lie among Hoy's Sitka spruce
the earth a bed of welcome.

Soft ground yields to my yawning form
mounds of memory stretch back.

Patches of sky
blur the high branches
where dreams of longing return...

Sleeping outside
in British Columbia
horizons shaped by mountains
bears lurk behind trees.

Sitting round the campfire
the kerosene lamp attracting moths
like lost souls disturbed in slumber
magnetised by light.

The smell of Cedar wood burning
chopped carefully from kindling.
Waves of orange on black rise
before embers fade into night...

The sun shifts and so do I.
Pine needles jag
return and repeat
memories
in a planted forest.

# Sunshine in the Hope

*for Christina Sargent*

A bright blue day on the bus
Then you greet me from a blue van
blasting Beethoven:
stacked with books and DVDs
a high shelf full of pots
seats down for sleeping.

We drive to the shore
walk among liquid mirrors.
Your sunlight smile
bandana red hair
like 1970s tie-dyed.

You show me a tapestry of birds
woven in silk.
We lunch with your family
in a sundrenched living room,
food in dishes placed on the coffee table.

The sound of geese beckons us outdoors.
They fly on the edge of your landscape view
as if placed there by some artist.

Birds thrive in your studio:
sketches of species in brown and yellow
gannets watching from dyed-green muslin
feathers outlined in dark pencil
spill from your book.

The clock strikes three
and you drive me back
to the blue day outside –
warm, like spring,
winter forgotten in February.

# Migration

SWALLOWS

## Carola Huttmann

# A Sense of Belonging

Born in a land where twilight
lasts the blink of an eye

where snow happens
but once a lifetime

where the Protea
is the national flower

where the sweeping landscape
meets the horizon.

It is where my heart
lingers still.

Ripped from all that
was familiar and right

I was transported
to the other side of the world,

to a country and people
I neither liked nor understood.

Adrift from the place that
had been home for so long

I was a pebble lost in a
vast sea of strangeness,

searching in vain
location after location

where I might gain once more
some sense of belonging.

Stepping out of the void
I came ashore on a tranquil island

very different from anything I'd
known before, yet strangely intimate,

replacing something long absent, its
space and sense of history sang out to me.

Here in this dreamland of merry dancers
and never-ending summer nights

I finally found the rest and
contentment I so badly sought.

# A Very Different Kind of Life

It was my twenty first birthday and I had never seen snow. As I tentatively stepped out of the airport building onto the runway of Aberdeen Airport, to walk the few steps to the waiting aircraft, the snow came down thick and fast, covering my hair and the shoulders of my new coat like fine lace. No one had told me it was going to feel like this -- magical. I looked at the other passengers making their way to the plane. They all had their heads bent against the snowflakes floating down to meet them as if in greeting. Well, they'd probably seen snow more times than they cared to remember, but I lifted my face to feel the flakes gently touch my skin like a velvet glove, before they melted away.

Three days before Christmas and I was making the journey from South Africa to Orkney. My purpose, to trace my great grandfather's footsteps and to find my grandfather who, I believed, may also have gone there many years before.

My grandfather and I had a lot in common. We had the same name, the same birthdays and I knew from what my father had told me that, like myself, he was a keen traveller with an unquenchable curiosity and a desire for knowledge about the world around him. He was a restless soul, never staying anywhere for long. He lived with my grandmother in a small house not far from us, but he would take off on one of his adventures with barely any notice and we wouldn't hear from him for months on end, sometimes even years.

The longest I remember him being away was three years. Mostly we didn't even know where he went. Very occasionally a postcard arrived from some exotic destination, bearing only a few words of greeting. He would return just as suddenly and unannounced as he'd left, undertaking a few jobs prospecting for gold, as his father had done before him. For a while, he and Grandmother would be like a couple of newlyweds. She didn't seem to begrudge his long spells away from home or that she'd had to bring up their son on her own. She said it kept their marriage fresh and gave her freedom and independence she wouldn't otherwise have had. As a young girl I remember being thrilled by the unusual gifts my grandfather brought back from his travels and fascinated by the stories he told.

"Did you *really* ride a camel through the Sahara?"

“I did indeed. And an uncomfortable ride it was too, on occasion.” Grandfather seemed delighted by how much his tales enchanted me.

From an early age I knew I wanted to be like him -- an independent spirit, unfettered by rules and conformity. I can still hear my mother’s words as she sighed:

“You’re just like your grandfather.”

Even though I so rarely saw him I felt an inexplicable bond with him which grew ever stronger as I grew older. It was this bond and the overwhelming desire to get to know my grandfather better -- almost as vital as the need to eat and drink -- that was taking me to such a remote corner of the world. I felt sure that meeting him again would give me a greater understanding of who I was.

The flight from Aberdeen to Orkney was quite short and soon we came in to land. The lights framing the runway beckoned to us as the plane made one last sweeping circle before we landed with hardly a bump.

Just days before I started my journey I’d found an advert on the internet.

> *Orkney couple, off to spend Christmas in New Zealand, seek to let their town house for a six-week period. Interested parties please get in touch for more information.*

The taxi driver dropped me off in a quiet street. With electric excitement I looked around at the dark outlines of a few scattered houses. Most of them had pretty lights in the windows. Then I spotted the little cottage looking somewhat out of place amongst the more modern buildings and was immediately drawn to it. I found the keys underneath the flowerpot next to the front door, just as the email had said. I walked into my new temporary home and stood for a moment, taking everything in. The house was much bigger than it looked from the outside and seemed perfect. There was even a real Christmas tree, elegantly decorated in reds and gold and homemade cookies on the coffee table.

In spite of being worn out from my long journey I spent that first evening transported back to being the little girl which used to sit on Grandfather’s knee as I read his diary. My grandmother had given me the beautiful leather-bound book just before I stepped onto the plane in Johannesburg.

“Happy Christmas. I hope this will help you in your quest”, she’d

whispered into my hair. "If you find him, give him a kiss from me."
The accounts of my grandfather's travels were pretty sketchy, nor did he explain why he didn't settle anywhere for long, but I hoped the diary would eventually give me some insight into the man I felt so close to, but about whom I knew so little.

The following morning I explored the small town of Kirkwall which formed the heart of this archipelago of islands. I quickly located the library – the oldest in Scotland, apparently – and spent the afternoon happily ensconced in its dusty archive room looking through old newspapers. Like a nagging headache the same questions kept bothering me. Had my grandfather stayed here for long? Had he found his father? Had either of them done anything noteworthy which local reporters might have written about?

The distinguished looking gentleman in charge was very apologetic when he came to tell me it was closing time. I returned to the cottage feeling mentally drained. My head spun with all the reading I had done. Passing a shop selling fish and chips I remembered hearing about this great British tradition and suddenly realised just how hungry I was. The generous piece of fish looked delicious and was wrapped in old newspaper before being handed to me over the counter. I couldn't wait to get it home.

I was about to crumple the paper into a tight ball and throw it away when, like a thunderbolt, it occurred to me that the meal I had just eaten had been packaged in a piece of history. I looked at the date. It was almost two years old. I idly glanced over the headlines. Then I saw it. I read it twice to make sure I wasn't dreaming.

*Prospector's Cottage Destroyed In Storm*, said the headline. I read on. The article related how, during the most severe gale the tiny island of Flotta had experienced in living memory, a lonely dwelling, known as *Prospector's Cottage*, set on a small hill just above the sea, had been wrecked. Its owner, known to the locals only as Sam, had been washed down the embankment whilst trying to secure the roof with tarpaulin. Although the lifeboat and local fishermen, risking their own lives, had searched the sea and shoreline they'd been unable to locate him. Three months later his body had been washed up several miles down the coast.

I hardly slept at all that night. My mind was a live wire of different emotions. Was it even remotely possible the article was about my grandfather? If it was, what a tragedy that I hadn't undertaken this trip before. Or did the report concern my great grandfather? Like his son, he liked to be different. He may well have made himself known by his old trade in places where he felt comfortable enough to settle for a while.

I practically ran to the library the next morning. The archivist was kind enough to take my state of mixed anxiety and excitement seriously and told me what he knew. Since the mid 1970s oil processing had been the mainstay of the Island and for the first decade Flotta had prospered.

"The flare burning off gasses from the refinery can be seen for miles around and must never be allowed to go out."

"It's possible, then, that my great grandfather might have found work at the terminal?" I mused aloud. The archivist agreed it was a possibility.

The next day I took the old car ferry to Flotta. Despite the stinging cold I went up on deck and let the beautiful scenery pass me by. Winter sunshine enveloped the landscape in a surreal golden glow. As I stood at the railings I heard someone coming up the stairs behind me, but I didn't look round. Darkness would fall soon enough and I wanted to engrave this view on my mind to remember it for the rest of my days.

"I guess I'm not the only one mad enough to want to catch my death of cold up here."

Time stopped. The accent, the intonation with which those words were spoken took me back half a lifetime. The voice came to stand beside me and I looked up to see a gentleman of middle years dressed in an expensive looking coat. He was holding a map in his hand.

"I should probably have taken the earlier boat, seeing as I'm not sure where I'm going and it will soon be dark."

He put his hand in his coat pocket and took out a folded piece of paper. It looked like a newspaper cutting and a sense of déjà vu trickled down my spine.

"My father stayed here for a while, I think. Sadly we lost touch a long time ago and I believe he may have died before I was able to find him again."

Perhaps it was the look on my face that made him extend his hand to me.

"How impolite of me", he apologised. "I'm Sam."

"I'm Sam too, well Samantha, actually. I came here to find my grandfather."

I felt as if I'd been running up a steep hill and paused to catch my breath.

“I think I may have just found him”, I said softly, uncertain I could trust my voice.

Sam looked out at the heaving waves. He obviously hadn’t heard me above the rising wind.

“Samantha?” he said suddenly as if my words had taken time to register.

“Did you say your name is Samantha?”

I nodded.

“Tell me a little about yourself, please.”

Sam was looking intently at me now. I quickly told him how I believed my grandfather and maybe even my great grandfather had come here to find the original Orkney. I lived in Orkney, South Africa and the same sense of adventure they shared, had brought me here to find them.

Before I had even finished Sam was embracing me in a huge, and somehow strangely familiar, bear hug.

“Welcome back into my world, dear Samantha. I have often thought about you, wondering if you’re anything like your father. I guess it was my restless nature and my pride that prevented me from coming home to find out.”

His last words came out in a choked whisper. Hot tears running down my frozen cheeks came to rest on the dark velvet of my grandfather’s coat. We stood together on that cold, wind-swept deck for a long time while our emotions crashed in on us like the wild sea around us. Eventually Sam drew away. His voice was still slightly hoarse.

“Come with me to see the place where your great grandfather spent his final years.”

I didn’t need asking twice.

Darkness was beginning to fall as we disembarked from the ferry. Lights along the length of the quay welcomed us to this tiny island and to a new chapter in our lives. The coxswain, wearing a Santa’s hat, waved to us and our fellow passengers wished each other a merry Christmas. This was Christmas Eve and as we linked arms to walk up the pier it started snowing. Not in a thousand years could I have dreamt of a better Christmas. Whatever happened in the future, this day and the chance to be reacquainted with my grandfather was a treasure I would carry with me forever.

# Catherine Turnbull

## Dancing to the Same Tune

I waited in the wings, clutching the fiddle they had lent me to my chest. From the side of the stage I could see my family dancing to the tribal drumming, all bright costumes and pounding feet. It was my turn next, my job to play the Red River Jig while my people showed off their fancy footwork. In the dark hall there were three hundred in the audience and they were all my family, my father said. As I saw the faces my heart raced, I swallowed hard. I had to go on.

When I first heard about my relatives living five thousand miles away, I was excited, rather than frightened, as I am now. My father held his hand up to stop me leaving the table after breakfast one morning, six months ago.

"We have an invitation to travel to see our family in Scotland. It is getting paid for by the cultural exchange," he said.

I hadn't a clue what he was talking about.

"It is an exchange of culture between our First Nation and those of our relatives in Scotland."

"Who are these family people?"

He told me: "Long ago when my father's father's father's father was a young boy, he lived on an island in the ocean in a place called Orkney in Scotland. That's five thousand miles away.

"For many generations his family had farmed the land, growing crops to feed his children and to sell, in the same way as our family here. But one day a man who said he owned the land came along and told him he would have to move off, just like what happened to our people. So he left his home and found somewhere else to go so he could survive."

I wondered why we had never heard of these folk before.

"Where did he go?"

"He came here to Canada on a ship, all those thousands of miles. His job was to buy food from the native farmers to feed the men who traded in the fur from the beaver. While he was here he married a native girl and you and I are descended from his children."

"So, who is this other family in the faraway place?"

"They are the other children of his father. They are called Tait like us and all my life I have wondered who they are."

"But father, why have they waited so many years to find us?"

My father sighed running his fingers through his greying hair. "It is the way the world is. There are people who are related who never find each other across these vast tracts of land and history. We are very lucky that we have the chance to meet our family. And you, Sarah, can play a big part in this."

"How?"

"You are the next generation. You have a cousin, Joyce, twelve-years-old, just like you and she plays the fiddle too. I thought you could play the Red River Jig, you do it so well. You have an ear for the music."

I heard the men playing that jig at dances, their feet shuffling to the fast rhythm, their fingers flying. I listened till the tune was right in my head, its melody playing over and over. They think I can hear a tune and then play it. But it isn't really like that. I have to know a thing many times first, sneaking about and listening. Then I wake in the morning and I've got it.

Never mind all that. I practised the Red River Jig before we left for Scotland, so much my fingers bled.

I wondered about my cousin. Would I have to get on the stage alone or would she play alongside me? Would she be like me and watch and listen and play?

It took us two clear days to get from our house to my cousins. That was a miracle, father said. When our ancestor William Tait did it in reverse he spent many weeks travelling by ship across the ocean, by canoe down the lake and the Red River. Father said it was an amazing coincidence that we live in St Andrew's on the Red in Manitoba and were headed for St Andrew's parish in Orkney.

When we arrived on our fourth plane journey our family was waiting for us in Kirkwall. Father and Mother made a great to do in hugging them all and giving gifts like soapstone carvings and beaded chokers. I hung back a bit and so did Joyce. I was glad about this. It takes me a while to get to know folks; I like to listen and watch first. So I took a sneaky look at her. She was wearing jeans like me and a fleecy top. Her fair hair was tied back but some strands hung over her eyes.

I busied myself looking out the window at the green homeland of my ancestor. There was plenty of sky just like on the Red, and cattle, too. While our land is somehow kind and friendly, even when blanketed in snow, this place seems smoothed out where it has yielded to the violence of fierce winds; almost like it was a protest rather than surrender. After just a few minutes we parked outside a long stone house crouched down to weather the storms. The water was just a few yards from the front door. I've been downstream to Lake Winnipeg which is as wide as an ocean with water as far as you can see, but I've never seen waves crashing on the shore with such fury. I shivered and followed my family inside.

My father and Joyce's were soon talking about how mine fished for pickerel on the river and hers put down Creoles to catch crab. To my mind Creole is a kind of music or a way of cooking, but each to its own. The folks here seem backward in what father calls the Old Country. Our mothers talked about bannocks. Before I knew it we had plates of them served cold with rubbery cheese. But Mother soon put them right and we had them fried up like they should be.

All the while Joyce was hiding behind her hair.

"Why don't you girls go upstairs and Joyce can show you the bedroom. You must have loads to talk about," her mother said.

I heard the sigh and could relate to that.

"We're really looking forward to hearing you play your fiddle, Sarah," Joyce's mother added. "We've been told you are really good. Maybe you could teach Joyce one of your tunes."

I wanted to say that it wouldn't work like that; she'd have to figure it out for herself. But this wouldn't sound right. I made a face that could look like I was willing to give it a go.

Joyce was already half way up the stairs. I knew she was angered by her mother's praise of me. The bedroom was cold and a blast howled though the ill-fitting window. I put my bag down near the door, something stopping me from claiming the narrow bed by the wall. On Joyce's side of the room, clothes were strewn across the bed and CDs were dumped on the bedside table. There were seals painted on the blue walls, a creature I have only seen on nature programmes.

"I so love your seals," I said tracing the arc of a swimming body with my fingers.

There was no answer. I turned to see Joyce was ear-plugged into her i-Player and hadn't heard a word. She was rocking gently in a chair to a tune I couldn't hear, her eyes closed. I was dismissed. If I wanted to inhabit her space I had to do it silently and at a distance. Downstairs the family bonding was being played out with laughter and music that drifted up through the floor like warmth in the air.

I stepped towards the window. The water was no longer near the house but hundreds of yards out. I'd read about the tides you get in the ocean but had forgotten that every day the sea rises and falls twice. It left behind a wide circle of plants and little pools of glistening water. A great black bird stood on the pier, its wings outstretched as wide as a man is tall. I wished I could join him in worshipping the water and fly up into the mantle of grey sky or dive deep into the watery depths, casting our ripples.

What is the bird called? Are there seals on the beach? What makes that mournful cry above the house? And why won't you speak to me?

There would be no answers tonight. I crept underneath the quilt, pulling it over my head. I was curled up in a knot and shivering, not just from the cold. As the numbness began to seep away I took off half my clothes under the coverlet. I was not to blame. Joyce was to blame for missing an opportunity, as my father called it. My bed by the Red in my dark room in our log house was cold without me. I pulled the pillow over my head in Orkney to block out the cries of its birds. Instead I heard the soothing voice of my owl in the trees. Then I slept all night.

When I wakened the wind shrieked around the stone house. The bed beside mine was empty. Joyce stood where the big black bird had stretched his wings wide the evening before; she was a hooded figure bent small in the storm.

---

I waited on the stage clutching the fiddle they had lent me to my chest. The applause for the native dancing was long, but not long enough. There was a silence I had to fill. I took a deep breath, held my head high and I was there in the middle of the stage; alone. The spotlight on me. I couldn't see the people, not even out front. I knew Father and Mother were there, proud as anything. I couldn't see my cousin in the wing, but I felt her watching me, more than the hundreds of pairs of eyes in the audience. I picked up my fiddle. It's not easy to go from a stop-start into that upbeat jig and the first note is always the worst. But I felt my feet respond into that easy shuffle we do and soon my fingers, now healed from the bleeding, were flying. For a moment I was back on the Red playing its tune as it tumbled over the rapids; our native drums on the shore and my Scottish ancestor on the far bank with his fiddle. There was another sound too which cut in as the image of my river disappeared. It was the pounding of feet. Several hundred were shuffling round the floor. I'd have to play for a few more minutes yet. Third time round I finished to the whooping and hollering of my people and the clapping of the Orcadians.

I stepped to one side of the stage as Joyce came on, hair over her eyes, head down. But she didn't raise her fiddle to her shoulder. She lifted her gaze to the middle distance and began to sing Greenland Whaling Fishery.

*In eighteen hundred and forty four*
*On March the twentieth day*
*We hoisted a flag to our foretop mast*
*And for Greenland sailed away, brave boys*
*And for Greenland sailed away*

Pure notes captured the room, holding everyone still. I knew this song. But when she got to the verse after the whale capsizes the boat:

*Sad news, sad news to our captain came*
*Which grieved his heart full sore*
*At the losing of the poor apprentice boy*
*But the whale grieved him ten times more, brave boys*
*But the whale grieved him ten times more*

Our version is different. The captain is more upset about losing the boy than the whale is.

As the last echoes faded away my throat was dry as sand. Hers was as clean as the pools washed on the beach.

Before the applause could get started she lifted her fiddle to play another tune I have known all my life; the D Reel. Instinctively I walked towards her and lifted my bow, slowing down to her pace, willing my feet to stay planted firmly on the stage. And there we were, playing the dance together, our bows synchronised, our notes the same. The floor below began to pulsate as people grabbed unfamiliar partners and guided each other.

"What is the name of that big black bird and why does he stand outstretched? He's a bit creepy."

"That's the cormorant," said Joyce. "He has to dry his wings out after he's been swimming."

"And why do you have seals painted in your room?"

"We call them selkies. We have a story that when the selkie women come ashore they slip off their skins and they have long legs and are beautiful. They bewitch the human men and can even marry and have families. But if someone finds their selkie skins on the beach and destroys them they will be very unhappy and pine away for their lives at sea. They have to have the choice to be on land or go back to sea."

"We have a lovely Cree story about the birds. A father sent his son out to live in the wild on his own so he could learn to be wise. Every time the son thought he had learned what he needed to, his father sent him away again. One day the father went to look for his son and heard his voice talking to a woman inside his tent. But when he went inside all the father could see were two robins. The son had learned how to be happy and free as a bird with his loved one."

"So how did you know the same music as me?" asked Joyce.

"Our ancestor took his music with him to Canada. All this time we've been dancing to the same tune."

# David Lea

## Where I Return to Again and Again

Now my favourite place
Looking out upon the world;
Friends pass by and wave.

Our Orkney chair and the view from our window are increasingly important to me. I see a great sweep of our wonderfully varied landscape, changing through the seasons. Memories of my time working here for the Royal Society for the Protection of Birds and running Go-Orkney tours are special and I get a surge of pleasure when migrating birds fly overhead or visit our garden.

Fertile farmland dominates the view and I think of the underlying layers of sandstone from which our soil derives. Green fields of grass change with the seasons and in summer there are beef cattle, mostly black Aberdeen Angus, never far away: on the slopes of Wideford Hill I can watch Heathfield's dairy cows going in and out for milking. There are always sheep and the colour of the arable fields changes as they are ploughed, turning green as the barley grows, then pale brown when it ripens. The hilltops are dark with heather and, on clear days, I can see the mountain tops of Morven and Scaraben, 60 miles away in Caithness.

In May wild pansies appear in fields that are still bare forming huge patches of purple: wild northern marsh orchids appear on our lawn, fingers of colour reminding me of the wilder parts of our islands.

There is a mound in a field across the valley that stands out from the crops because it is never cultivated. A few years ago a tractor collapsed the top of the mound and work by archaeologists showed it was a Neolithic tomb, similar in type, though not in size, to the great tomb of Maeshowe, a few miles to the west. They discovered a light-box aligned with sunrise at the midwinter solstice: the magnificent tomb of Newgrange in the Boyne Valley in Ireland has one and I shall never forget my visit there some years ago. The rising and setting sun at midwinter will have highlighted the start of a new year to our ancestors. Recently another ancient tomb was found on the slope below Wideford Hill, due west from our home.

To the south is the central part of Scapa Flow, one of the greatest harbours in the world: so important to our history and our economy and for its wild birds. Across the water I see parts of the islands of Hoy, Fara and Flotta with the oil terminal and its permanent flare. The tankers come and go, some taking away the oil piped in from 140 miles out in the North Sea. Others come with vast loads from countries like Russia and transfer them to slightly smaller boats who take it off around the world; some loads can be worth a hundred million pounds.

When the oil terminal opened the number of oiled birds increased alarmingly. I became deeply upset and Government Agencies would not identify the source of the oil. I dumped a small heap of dead, oiled birds at Orkney Harbours office and took some to the home of our M.P., Jo Grimond. His wife, Laura, came to the door and said "David, do come in and have a cup of tea."! A few days later Jo walked into our house and asked for a sample of the oil which he took to a Government Minister. In a few hours it had been identified as tanker washings. Quite soon procedures were changed and there were far fewer oiled birds.

Laura became a friend of ours. I remember once taking Morton Boyd, the Scottish Director of the Nature Conservancy, to meet Jo but he was away. It was a totally still day and biting midges were everywhere. Laura stood on the doorstep looking smart in short socks and a sleeveless shirt while her visitor, wearing a kilt, tried to stop the midge bites becoming too bad. Laura ignored them and, as we got back into our car, Morton said he thought she must have a skin like leather.

Lying in front of our house are two joined whalebones we found in Birsay Bay. They remind me of the time we had four Sperm Whales, apparently trapped in Scapa Flow for a few months. We hired a boat to visit them and, later, watched them being herded out to the Pentland Firth; they needed the deep ocean in which to feed. It seemed that one was old and much paler than the others who were obviously caring for it.

On fine evenings I watch the setting sun. Around midwinter it sinks down over the Flow: at the time of the equinoxes it sets behind Braehead Farm and the tip of the TV mast on Keelylang: at midsummer it sets behind the Rendall hills. On bright mornings I like to watch the sunlight move down the hill.

In the three years we have lived in this house we have seen more than 70 species of birds and enjoyed them all. One morning, while we ate our breakfast, a peregrine flew by and, in spring, I sometimes watch ravens rolling in display.

It is good to think about the countries where some of our migrants come from. Last winter we had visits from a tiny Siberian Chiffchaff, feeding in the bushes close to my chair. I marvelled that such a tiny thing had crossed the North Sea and it was still with us in the snows of late February. Whooper Swans from Iceland have passed overhead and in summer Arctic Terns fly between Scapa and Kirkwall bays. A few months later they might be on the edge of the Antarctic pack ice, the greatest travellers in the world.

In the play area across the road there is sometimes a brown hare hiding in the grass. It spends the daylight hours crouching low, usually in the same spot which it must have stored in its memory. I need my binoculars to bring it into view. In early December a second hare was briefly here and they played together with a little boxing, a sign of pairing. In January a young one appeared.

Binoculars are an essential asset to my world. Not only can I check out the birds and the ships but also the people passing by. I like to sweep the sky and spot things invisible to normal sight. Just recently a black dot turned out to be a Bonxie, a Great Skua, which then flew over our house.

Over the years in our special community we have come to know many folk and when someone waves to me I realise what a lucky man I am.

## LC Littlejohn

# The Return

Then
she stood at windy bus stops
Now
in undercover palace
across a monitor
her destination flashes

Then
a place of slag heaps
black ski jumps
Now
an alien landscape
of level fields and plains
a green-ness
she cannot comprehend

Then
back-to-back houses
straight ribs off
a tarmac spine
Now
porches, conservatories
doors of red and green
belie what lies
behind.

Note: A return to urban West Yorkshire sparked off this poem.

# The Reunion

The invitation card was pushed to the back of the worktop but I knew it was there.

My eyes were like x-rays, exposing the wording through the dense wall of boxes and debris I had shored up in front of it.

**30th Reunion of Class of 1966**
**16 March**

It was bound to be disastrous. Did nobody realize that you couldn't go back and be the same, young, careless and carefree? For sure, we had been all three.

Yet life in the Nurses' Home was strict. Late passes to midnight were like gold dust. Home Sister, who missed nothing, watched for stray students with the dark beady eye of a mother mallard. Little did she know that, once the Cinderellas returned, they as quickly left their rooms and descended to the outside via spikes driven into the exterior of the west wall. These were considered the work of a beneficent builder.

We'd always meet in someone's bedroom for late night post-mortems. Laughter had been the answer to every blip and slip; like Mattie, in fright and haste, fixing the neuro-surgeon's headlight on back to front so that its beam shone uselessly out of his occiput. We laughed so much at the telling that our ribs ached, with Mattie striding about like a headless chicken, white cap awry, imitating the surgeon's stricken movements. Goodness, it seemed like yesterday.

I sat in front of my mirror, experimenting. No amount of make-up could hide all the lines and creases. Polyfilla might, I thought, mournfully, then brightened. At least I didn't wear glasses anymore and my teeth were straight…the final year photograph gazed back at me from the dressing table. Well, perhaps the specs were quite trendy at the time and the outfit was attractive. It still hung somewhere at the back of the wardrobe.

Ten pounds a month had been our student pay; pocket money really, since all board and food was found. Still, a tenner didn't last long, not when you swung off to the C & A store with your pals, determined to spend, spend, spend on dresses with wide skirts and net petticoats that mercilessly scratched the bare skin between stocking top and knicker bottom.

By the end of the month a meal had to be the cheapest possible and beans on toast fitted that bill. Then back to duty…

My hand holding the lipstick shook slightly. Theatre sister; everyone was terrified of her. Even the brightest in the class could be reduced to jelly. Grim of face and clipped in speech, she was known to lose her temper spectacularly with incompetent students. "Lift the instruments out of the sterilizer, Nurse, with forceps!" A perilous chore at the best of times, I'd promptly dropped the lot on the floor. How my knees shook … and my heart banged so much it seemed to leap about untethered under my ribcage. What would she say – or do?

Tch, tch. I snapped the lipstick back into its case and rose to go. No point in putting this off.

It was every bit as bad as I had feared: twenty women in their late fifties screaming at each other on recognition. Unseen, I'd paused in the doorway. Am I as old as they look? Surely not. Why had they put up all those big photographs, showing us so young, fresh and smooth of skin? My gaze moved from black and white reproductions of careless, beautiful youth to the roomful of thickened waistlines, desperate thinness and ageing faces.

"And what are *you* doing now, Lena?" She's talking to me. My mouth says something, my mind another.

"Really? I thought you'd be Chief Nurse to the Government by this time." Slight snigger… I wish dire consequences on her head.

Good heavens, it really was big Clara from the coastal village talking in that upper-class accent. What had happened to the clumsy, shy girl who found herself a student-nurse against all expectations from her fisher family? That one-time shy girl now loomed before me.

"Well, Lena," like a headmistress, "did your family go to university like mine?" Since James had determinedly refused all pressure from his teachers to do any such thing and Sarah had promptly got herself pregnant at seventeen, I smiled a rictus, and edged away.

At last it was all over. The photos had been taken, the dinner devoured (change places please, after each course, so that you can catch up with different people) and I could decently take my leave of this group of unrecognisable women. Where had they disappeared to, that band of responsible-irresponsible girls?

Safely in the metal cocoon of my car, I rest my hands on the steering wheel. The veins bulge slightly and one finger is misshapen with early arthritis. I lean my head on those hands and weep for lost youth.

## Margaret Storr

### Turnstone

The chill begins.
Ice sparkles and crackles underfoot.
The fledgling turnstone rises unwillingly,
Obeying information it cannot resist,
Wired genetically in its brain.
Home is where the nest was,
Where food was plentiful.
But icy seas and frozen Greenland
Must be traversed to reach freedom,
Far from the murdering Arctic cold.
Attrition rates mount high
Till Peter's Pool is gained at last.
Here, under the frost-free slimy seaweed,
Storm-piled high on the foreshore,
Lie feasts of plump invertebrates;
More delicacies under each turned stone.
Enough food, then, to pile on the fat
Till May calls the bird home again
Across the perilous seas to Arctic Ellesmere;
To nest, to mate, to reproduce.
The cycle starts once more.

The chill begins.
Glass sparkles and crackles underfoot.
The fledgling Iudit rises unwillingly,
Obedience to parents
Wired socially in her brain.
Home was safe and warm,
Food and family plentiful.
Clattering now over rhythmical rails,
Sleepless nights and days she endures
In a bid to reach freedom,

Far from the murdering grip of inhumanity.
Attrition rates mount high.
Iudit survives; safety is reached at last.
Here in unfamiliar, bomb-scarred London,
Rations just adequate, new friends are made.
She grows, now Judith, to mature, nest, mate and
    reproduce.
First come her children.
Then, turning the stones of memory,
She finds pictures and stories.
Memory calls her back again,
To seek where home is.
Unlike the bird, she finds it,
Not where it once was,
But where she built her nest.
The cycle starts once more.
Fledglings now flown, she nests again,
Her new mate her memories,
Her new progeny her books.

# Twitchy Waters

They squat, two men, sights fixed on the shore below.
A third stands away, behind a bush, his telescope
Fixed on its tripod, ready, focused, like him.
Cameras are hidden all around.

A slight movement among the heaps of kelp and bladderwrack.
"Look there!" whispers one; the other nods excitedly.
"Keep still, you fool, don't draw attention to yourself."
"We'll get the buggers yet," both think.
"Distinction within our group."
"One for my records."
"Bloody brown bastards!" mutters the leader. "This wind's a killer."
"Grey, it says here in my notes, not brown."
"Mine says brown; shut up!"

The heavy sky leaches out colours.
In the gloom, a flash explodes.
The slimy shore erupts with bodies, squat, brown, grey.
Squeaking like mice, one wing uplifted they run to and fro,
Yellow-stockinged, but unlike Malvolio,
Not cross-gartered.
Then panic forgotten,
The crowd on shore makes for the sea's brim,
Stabbing for molluscs, hopping the wavelets,
Running back from the threatening tide.

Away from the cliff's edge, no silence now.
"You fool!" the leader shouts. "I said no flash!"
"I'm sorry," comes the mumble. "It was dark."

"And how will we now get good pictorial proof
To take back to the club? Our plane leaves soon -
We've lost our edge back home.
These purple bastards are not the same as ours down south.
Different beaks and they come from God knows where."

"Purple sandpipers? What purple?" comes a grumble.
"Dreary brown, I say."
"No, grey!"
"Where do they come from?"
"Why don't you know?"
"What's the mystery?"
"Mystery? How romantic!"

"Too small!" he shouts at them.
"Those yellow legs, too slight
For satellite tracking tags.
God, what a cock-up!"

*Just a bit more techno-know-how,*
Mutters the leader to himself.
*Then we'll nail them.*
*Numbers, sex, colour, weight, size,*
*Bases here on our shores –*
*All known.*
*We must have country of origin.*
*Mystery?*
*Dangerous, romantic nonsense.*

# Imagined Landscapes

BONXIE (Great Skua)

# Lynn Johnson

## Boderan

The woman was dead.

Boderan crept around the Healer's body, noting the open, unblinking eyes, the leg turned outward where no joint allowed such movement, and the blood of life, dark and set around her head like a dried up river bed.

Boderan had not called this woman mother for many years; the village had willingly undertaken that role to spare their healer so that she may spend time communing with the gods for their benefit.

Early on Boderan had learned to take second place to the village - far more important than one girl child, even though that child was their future, their next healer, without whom the village would die.

With the lightest of touches she closed the staring eyes. The cold skin had seen many winters and had the feel of a well cured animal skin. She returned the leg to a natural position of rest. The Healer had not lain at the foot of the rocks too long but was, even now, on her way to the ancestors.

The sun moved across the sky. Boderan watched the clouds making shapes she could not yet read. There was still much to learn. Too much.

She placed her hand on her mother's heart willing it to life even as she knew the beat had gone forever. She had not expected to take her mother's place so soon. Already the burden felt too great, more powerful than the thoughts of death soaked into this place.

She trembled. The hairs on her arms prickled as if they had been touched by an unseen hand.

'*The eyes! Look at the eyes!*'

Whispers caught in a gust of wind. But there was no-one.

The sun sank in the sky. Soon she must return to the village so she could guide them back to this spot before dark. Her mother would need help to complete her journey to the House of the Dead.

She placed the cold hands together and laid them over The Healer's heart and got to her feet. Her stiff legs almost gave way but she forced them forward.

'*Seek the truth.*'

She spun round to follow the voice, but it was everywhere. Calling.

And then, nothing.

Emptiness.

Once the village knew The Healer lived no more, her own life would never be the same again. If the walk back had been longer there would have been time to adjust, but whispered words held little comfort, and when she reached the village the panic within was so strong she could scarcely breathe.

The Head Man picked her out as she entered the hearths as if he had been waiting for her. She knelt on the grass before him and told her story.

She had expected to accompany The Healer on her morning gathering of herbs and medicines so she might discover the favourite growing grounds of the rarer plants. Instead The Healer commanded her to remain behind to complete the drying out of yesterday's gatherings so there was room for the new supplies. Having completed her tasks Boderan had walked out to meet her.

She could not continue. The loss was too great and she was unworthy. Would the spirits test her? How would she know when the sick were ready to meet the ancestors?

A tap on her shoulder. She raised her head and read the pain on the Head Man's face through water-filled eyes.

'You say the body was without life? The Healer's spirit chose to leave us?'

'She had fallen from the rocks and her leg was broken, but a blow to the head took her life. Her spirit had started out on its last journey before I got to her.'

She didn't tell him of the horror she had seen in the eyes of The Healer who must have seen death walking towards her. That The Healer's spirit had been helped on its journey by something, or someone, evil.

There were no footsteps even though she had searched for signs on her knees. She had climbed to the top of the rocky place looking for any small detail, a clue of what had taken place.

Then she saw it, the palm-shaped stone with blood on one side telling her the Healer's death was not a result of her carelessness, and that she may have even joined the ancestors before her body had hit the ground. If only Boderan had disobeyed her mother's instructions, she would have been at her side and maybe the evil one would not have claimed her.

The Head Man nodded as if he had heard the words unspoken. He smiled and rose before her. Now that the time had come, a calmness descended on her. She felt his hand on her head, firm and strong, and his words proclaiming her Healer, seemed distant. Then he bade her rise and called for aid from the men who worked within the village boundaries.

They made haste and she walked beside him as befitted her new status. The Shaman came with them, walking on her throwing side. He would make the final preparations for the body and preside over the formal ceremony to make her Healer.

When they drew close to the body the Head Man looked at her sharply, but did not speak. Boderan was sure he had read the story of the Healer's last moments as surely as if the body itself had spoken to him. He nodded to her. She would have to explain why she had told no-one - but not here, not now.

Everyone waited. The Shaman moved close. He closed his eyes, and asked permission of the gods to move the Healer. The men waited.

When his eyes opened, the Shaman was looking directly at Horag, the oldest among the men. Horag came forward and carefully laid The Healer upon the deer skin they had placed in readiness and motioned the rest forward to stand at each corner. So it was they left that place, The Shaman calling upon The Healer's spirit to accompany them on the journey.

They made slow progress and she had more than enough time to consider what had happened. The more she thought about that look on The Healer's face, the more convinced she became that her spirit had not left voluntarily.

Boderan returned to The Healer's hearth as the last of the sun disappeared below the land. She uncovered the grooved bowls containing ceremonial wine. Yes, there would be plenty for tonight.

'*Seek the truth.*'

The words echoed in her ear, but she was alone.

Did the idea come from the voice, or had it lingered in the back of her mind all along? She couldn't be sure, but now she knew what she had to do.

She macerated ergot and dropped some into each bowl. No-one would notice in the frenzy of the ceremony. The guilty person would make himself known tonight.

Boderan was small for her age. Others who had passed as many summers were taller and swifter, and their eyes keener. But she could see with her fingers, could tell the life-giving plants from those bringing sickness and deep sleep. And when someone was sick, her fingers told her what was wrong. That was her mother's gift to her. And now, that must be the gift she will pass on to her own girl child.

The ceremony to mark The Healer's journey to the Land of the Dead would take place tonight. After the setting of one sun, the Healer would take the sacred path to join her ancestors at Unstan Tomb where no doubt she will be as welcome in death as she had been in life.

The Head Man was standing close to Horag whispering words for his ears only. Horag the Brave had lead many hunts and was well thought of. Now, he held his cutting stone high above his head and there was much anger in his body.

Boderan was curious, but knew they would stop their men's talk if she joined them. But, she did have good reason.

She picked the bloodied stone out of her bag, surprised again by its weight, too big to be held in the palm of her small hand. The stone held battle scars and it must have been a large man who could wield it easily.

She made her way to where they stood, beyond the hearths, in the black shadows.

'I found this.' She handed over the stone. No other words were necessary.

The Head Man took it. It was too large even for his hands. Boderan had already discounted the women and children, and most of the men. Few could have used such a tool.

The Head Man's eyes challenged her to give the story an ending, but she wasn't yet ready. Again he appeared satisfied even though she had not spoken.

He moved to the centre by the hearth and in the flames his face was unreadable.

'We must make ready for the journey to the House of the Dead.' He clapped his hands and the first of the night's stories began.

Everyone had a tale to tell of The Healer who had entered each of their lives at some point and exited almost without them knowing. She calmed them, helped them to sleep, and took away their pains with her magic. Many feared her, especially those who had been dragged back from their journey to the ancestors, knowing she had fought with the gods for their return. All the Healer would say was that the time was not yet right, otherwise the gods would not have given in.

One man was not afraid. The shadow of Horag stood beside the Head Man head and shoulders taller and, with little meat on his bones, he looked different from the others. He had not mated, although he was entering the last years of his life. His interests had lain, not in giving new life, but in ordering his fellow hunters.

He was arguing with the Head Man now and Boderan watched his movements with interest. He flung out his arm and, pointing south, asked to be the hunter sent to attend the next village. Their Healer would come for a while to finish Boderan's training and in return Boderan's village must send a warrior with a strong arm to help in the fight against evil.

'You are a good hunter, Horag, but you are too old. You will be an insult to our friends. We have to send a fine young hunter to make up for the loss of their Healer.'

Horag was not convinced. His face paled and Boderan thought he looked less angry, more anxious.

All was ready. Boderan spoke to the Head Man and he called everyone to form a circle so that no spirit should feel excluded, he said.

Boderan walked three times around the outside of the circle. The wine looked no different than usual as she filled their drinking vessels. Gradually the laughing and chatter fell silent. All eyes were upon her, some anxious, not knowing what was coming.

She started to hum and they followed, heads moving in unison. In a low voice she spoke the magic words she said had been told to her by The Healer. The more they tried to concentrate, the quieter she spoke. Then suddenly she raised her voice and it came out deep and clear, not like her own voice at all.

'Who among us has committed the terrible sin of deciding when a spirit should be taken away? Who among us thinks he is a god that he can determine when and how The Healer should walk with the ancestors?'

Many looked uncomfortable, wishing to take their leave, but their bodies were no longer their own. Deliberately, she stopped and placed a hand on each shoulder, as if communing directly with their spirits. Last of all she stopped at Horag, placing first one and then her second hand on his sagging shoulders. She captured his spirit with the strength of her own, her eyes burning into his soul until he could no longer bear to look at her. He dropped his head as she pronounced his guilt, not shocked, only defeated.

She clapped her hands and it seemed to the villagers that they were waking from a deep sleep. Horag jumped to his feet but others had witnessed his actions and were swift to stop him. They bound his legs with gut so he could not leave. Before he knew what was happening, the circle closed around him.

'Horag, you have been found guilty of this deed. How do you answer to the charge?'

'I had to find a way to leave the village...' His voice broke. He covered his face like he was weeping. 'I had to leave, I had to.'

His voice became stronger and he lifted his head, 'I didn't know how to leave and was afraid to stay. I want my own hearth, a family of hunters I can be proud of. I knew that if The Healer was dead we would have to send a warrior to another village in exchange. There, I could build a new life. My spear has been raised many times to help my fellow men, but now my life here has no meaning.' His head bowed and he could not hide his shame.

'You, Horag, have done a terrible deed.' The Head Man's voice was gruff and his eyes were not without compassion. 'You have killed a woman of your village. Not only that, you have killed The Healer whose death could raise the evil ones who seek to destroy our village with sickness and despair.

'We cannot kill you for you could meet the Healer on your own journey to the House of the Dead. You will not be welcome there and you are not welcome here. Instead, you will be cast out with nothing. You will have only the company of the gods who still walk with you. If it is their will, you may yet find a village in another place where you may rest and make your home.'

They stripped him of his weapons and charms, and left only the skins he wore to keep out the chill of the night. All knew a lone hunter was unlikely to survive, even with his weapons. Then the Head Man pointed towards the place where the sun had gone to sleep. 'Be gone, you are no longer of this village.'

Horag was about to speak but the Head Man pointed to the sky. 'From this time onwards you are not part of this village. You are as nothing to us.'

Horag knew he was defeated. He glanced at Boderan as he walked away from the circle to the darkness beyond. The tears in her eyes met the hate and anger in his. Then, he melted into the darkness.

The Head Man turned and placed his hand in hers. 'You are already powerful, Healer. You are your mother's daughter and have little to learn, but the healer we have sent for will give you guidance, until you are ready to take your rightful place at The Healer's hearth.'

She wanted to tell him she hadn't done anything. That the potion she had made only sent people into a light daze, that the incantation was just a story told to her by The Healer as they went about their tasks.

Until she remembered The Healer's words; the healer's most powerful quality is silence.

She thanked the Head Man for his words of praise. The time for silence had come.

# Mandy Haggith

## Chambered Cairn (NC 24051450)

a shrine tumbles up from 5000 years or so ago
into this breezy secular present

stones offer a threshold
where dead and living cross over

a territory edge to wonder
where understanding might begin

## New Moon Cairn

I take care of the moon shrine. It is a quiet place. It is less grand than the sun temple or the shrine to the harvest spirits, but I think it is more beautiful.

They call it the grey tomb, some of them, mostly men who have never been inside. There is nothing grey about this place. It is white and red, like the moon and like a womb. It is a safe place. We smile, we laugh, we sing. We cry too, but sometimes it is helpful to cry. And always it is good to sit together, without speaking, in the darkness. It is always good to be quiet.

I have become familiar with all the nuances of quietness, its many mysteries. I will never tire of them. Chatter, livestock, the sound of running water: leave them elsewhere.

Inside the shrine, within the cairn, there can be silence deeper than the night sky. Instead of stars, flames. There is a particular quiet when a flame is put out. That particular quiet is good. It is powerful, but not harmful, not evil, not if treated with respect. It can be scary, that's true. I have known many women to be afraid when a flame snuffs out, especially in here. Flames are life and the way back to life for those who have lost their way. We help them back, just as we help the moon to come back, when it thins away to nothing and needs our songs to give it strength to grow again.

Women come here to make requests or to plead for a kick inside the womb, but mostly to remember. Perhaps because I am alone I am able to intercede on their behalf with those we cannot name. We never talk about my solitude. We never do, never. I speak only about them. I try to become invisible and simply inhabit the quiet space where they come to grieve, to pour out their sorrow for their lost children. I offer them a vessel, that is all.

I have seen so many women mourning unborn daughters or those taken too soon, before they could cry for their mother, the unheard, silent births, the still ones. They bring bones of infants laid to the earth without being weaned. Some have died in ways that are rumoured to be unkind, some have been put out to starve because they are crippled, six-fingered or twinned. I take the bones anyway and I ask no questions. The moon shines on us all and her movements are unperturbed by storms, famines or pestilences. I must be as she is. So they bring me the bones of their children and I take care of them all.

And I watch the moon.

---

There is no moon tonight. She is lost from us. This is the time women come to the shrine.

They arrive, one by one and in little groups, and wait for the darkness of evening. Some have walked far. In the gloaming, we light the rush wicks of our lamps. Sisters and mothers share, gathering around one flame. It is good to share.

I remember my first time. My aunt was the caretaker back then. I came with my mother and my sister and we huddled around one flame, hands held in a triangle to protect the memory of my brother. He was dead then, but now he is back among us: my sister has him for a son, a fine boy. This is why we have this shrine. Without it, how would the children be able to cross back over the threshold?

At first there is banter among the women, and laughter, especially from the girls, as they take off their clothes and give me the bundles to keep them dry. It is cold tonight, the wind is from the east, so I waste no time. Once all the lamps are lit and we are all bare-skinned, I lead the way in. It is a simple cairn: there is no outer chamber or long passage. We must stoop to enter and, crouching inside, our flames turn the quartzite walls to moon-glow white.

I position my light on the shelf to make the red roof-stones shine, then sit in the hollow at the back with my drum, patting its belly, so it laughs everyone inside. We sit in a circle and push the lamps closer and closer together until they form a tight ring at our centre. The shrine glows like milk and blood.

I ask them all to hold hands as I say a blessing. I have made a sweet potion of milk and moonwort in the whalebone beaker we use to awaken our memories. I pass the memory cup to the girl on my right and she sips and hands it on. We sing the memory song. Then I open the casket. All the things the women have brought me are in it, and I pass them one by one: this month there is a tiny boot of soft kid-skin. When it reaches the fourth woman in the circle, she sighs and speaks about her daughter. We listen, and then she passes it on. Everyone touches the little empty foot, handling it gently, and when it returns to me I lay it on the stone shelf. Some of the objects bring forth no comment. Some are spoken to by many.

When the casket is empty I close it. The moon cup is refilled and we sing the moon song as it is passed around. I beat the heart drum. I drum the beat of hearts. A drum, a beat, a heart. The flames die one by one. I drum until they all go out. When only my lamp burns under the red roof stones, I stop drumming and kill its flame.

Darkness and quiet. It is always good to be quiet

listening

hushed breath

shuffle of the dead

a move inside a womb

The dead and living mingle, passing back and forth through the opening we have made. Seeing nothing, our other senses wake up.

I hold the unborn skull in my left hand and listen to its silent howl. Then I pass it to my left, setting it free to undo the circle. Closing my eyes, I listen to its passage around the shrine, a wave of sorrow as the unnamed ones unleash themselves among us.

When the cold dome of the unborn reaches me again I pass it on to my left and it circulates once more. Sometimes this second wave is wilder than the first, but tonight it is less intense.

When it returns to me, I feel that the small bone moon is warmer. I send it around again and this time it manages to gather up all of the sobs as it passes. I have known it to take many rounds to mop up all the tears in the shrine but tonight three turns are enough.

The small hand on my right passes me the skull and silence is restored. The unborn knows it is not alone. The moon knows its way home.

Soon I shall begin the womb song, but for now we sit, because it is good to sit in the darkness, in quiet. It is always good to be quiet.

# Anna Lipinska

## The Song of a Beating Heart

The woman cried, water running down her face like the burn after rain. When the man came to the hearth he found her sobbing. It was almost like the times when the babies came and pain tore at her body. When she could at last speak, she showed him the pot, cracked down one side. Now she would have to make another and he knew that of all the jobs she did, it was the most difficult for her.

He sat looking into the fire. As he rested on his rock, the scented, swarming smoke calmed him. The smell meant warmth, food and light to him. There were other pots on the stones behind him. He knew they were there. She knew they were there. But women liked their pots and got used to them. Pots were good friends- you worked hard for them and they worked hard for you.

If she was in the place where she cried and worried about the effort of making a new pot, then he could not be happy and calm. She was a good woman who made food taste good, bore good strong children, (mostly boys, which pleased the man). But her unhappiness would become his unhappiness. His work in the field or his hunting and fishing would be spoiled. He would have to come back with the failing light to see her and hear her. He would have to find a way out of this or he would not know peace.

He told her not to break the pot until he came back again. He knew that she would obey – he was tall and strong, and was good at providing food – she could not find a better man. He bent to leave his building and pulled his hide cloak around his shoulders. His tough hide foot coverings made a shushing sound as he strode to the other building; going to one picked out like a right arrow to a fat tasty bird.

The woman there was without a man but had good children. The other women too would give her food and help with the scraping and chewing of hides to soften them. This woman had lost her man many harvests ago when he did not come back from finding fish. Looking after this woman was a way the others had of asking the skies to help them keep their own men with them.

He carried with him a piece of meat, a big piece which would feed her family well. He had killed the male ox himself rather than feed it over the long cold nights when little grew. The meat had hung above the fire in the smoke that gathered under the turf roof of his own building. It would be good eating.

He knew that if he gave her this he could ask for a pot in exchange. That would make his woman happy, too. The woman with no man was good at making pots and would enjoy the meat. He thought that this way, all would be happy. He could come back from the field to a good fire, and good meat but most of all, good peace.

He gave his woman the pot and watched as her face changed. He knew all would be well.

Taking the cracked pot from the woman, he wet a freshly chewed hide and stretched it across the pot. He tied the hide in place with a wet thong and put the pot in his sleeping place beside the fire.

When the light was going away he came back from the waters with fish to eat. The woman was happy still and so he was happy too. He picked up the cracked pot with its new covering and tapped the hide with his fingers. The noise was good to him; he tapped faster like the tapping in his chest.

# Taking Flight

# Ron Ferguson

## GEORGE MACKAY BROWN
## The Wound and the Gift

### PROLOGUE

*History is fiction that* did *happen. Whereas fiction is history that* might have *happened.* – Andre Gide

*America is the only country in the world where not to promote yourself is seen as a sign of arrogance. – Garry Trudeau.*

It's one of those still, seraphic June evenings that Orkney throws up surprisingly frequently. This has been a benediction of a day. My wife, Cristine, and I have had a meal out here on the decking of our wooden Norwegian house down by the coast at Orphir, looking out to the blue hills of Hoy. A few hundred yards farther along the shore stands a ruined manor house, once the home of Orkney's famed Arctic explorer John Rae, discoverer of the North West passage and creator of a coruscating Victorian scandal.

The phone rings from time to time throughout the evening. We talk to our three grown-up children, Fiona, Neil and Ally, and to our two little grandchildren, Olly and Dan. The cows are lowing in the field next to our house, Bach's Mass in B Minor is on the CD player, and I've a glass of Orkney's 12-year-old single malt Highland Park in my hand. It's only a day or two after June 21$^{st}$, when the sun reaches its northernmost point and we start to head slowly but inexorably towards the long and sometimes bleak darkness of a Northern winter. But that's a long way off Although it's nearly 10pm, and the orange disc of the sun is touching the horizon, the light is still strong enough for me to read an exquisitely written book.

Life doesn't get much better.

It was George Mackay Brown's *An Orkney Tapestry* which attracted me to these islands nearly a quarter of a century ago. Its strange power has drawn many visitors-turned-residents, including one of the greatest living composers, Sir Peter Maxwell Davies. I'm reading it now for the third time, and it still affects me. This most peculiar guide to Orkney is, literally, a fabulous book. It has history, of sorts, but also stories and poems and dramas. The back cover says that the author "explores the dark mysterious corners, as well as the quiet beautiful fertile places, in his search for the still point of Orkney's history, the true face of the Orkney Fable." Brown says that most writers about Orkney have been practical in their approach. He is doing something different. His manifesto is intriguing.

> *This book takes its stand with the poets. I am interested in the facts only as they tend and gesture, like birds and grass and waves, 'in the gale of life'. I have tried to make a kind of profile of Orkney, which is not a likeness of today only; it has been worked on for many centuries.... The facts of our history – what Edwin Muir called The Story – are there to read and study: the Neolithic folk, Picts, Norsemen, Scots, the slow struggle of the people towards independence and prosperity. But it often seems that history is only the forging, out of terrible and kindly fires, of a mask. The mask is undeniably there; it is impressive and reassuring, it flatters us to wear it.*
>
> *Underneath, the true face dreams on, and The Fable is repeated over and over again.*

Hmmm. This is a strange beast. The true face dreams on? What on earth does he mean by that? What is Orkney's flattering mask all about? What is it that is being covered up? This bardic tale begins with the physical approach to the Orkney islands, from the port of Scrabster, on the rugged coast of northern Scotland.

> *There is the Pentland Firth to cross, first of all. This is looked on as a fearsome experience by some people who are visiting Orkney for the first time. In Scrabster they sip brandy or swallow sea-sick tablets. The crossing can be rough enough - the Atlantic and the North Sea invading each other's domain twice a day, raging back and fore through the narrow channels and sounds, an external wrestle; and the fickle wind can be foe or ally. But as often as not the Firth is calm; the St Ola dips through a gentle swell between Scrabster and Stromness.*

> *George Bernard Shaw visited Orkney once in the nineteen-twenties. He was impressed by that mighty outpouring of waters. There was power enough in the Pentland Firth, he wrote, to provide all Europe with electrical power. A pair of millstones at the bottom of the Firth grind the salt that makes the sea the way it is; the maelstrom called The Swelkie whirls above the place where the querns forever turn (or so the old people believed).*
>
> *The cliffs of western Hoy rise up, pillars of flame. This coast has some of the tallest cliff-faces in the world, St John's Head, The Kame, The Berry, Rora Head: magnificent presences. There among them, standing out to sea a little, is the rock-stack called The Old Man of Hoy; very famous now since a team of climbers tackled it before television cameras in 1967, and got to the summit after sleeping a night in the bird-fretted crannies. An imposing presence; but from some aspects the Old Man looks comical, with his top hat and frock coat, like a Victorian gentleman, the last of the lairds turning his back on Orkney.*

I look over to Hoy again. I'd never thought of the familiar Old Man as a Victorian laird. Good writing makes you look at the world differently. Good whisky sometimes does that too. Another sip of Highland Park.

George Mackay Brown is clearly awed by the sense of history in the islands. The first Orkney peoples, he says, can only be seen darkly, a few figures on a moorland against the sky, between twilight and night. They are beyond the reach of legend even. Hardly a thing is known about Orkney's first inhabitants, says Brown, apart from the monuments they left behind them: the huge stones of Maeshowe and Brodgar, and the pastoral village of Skara Brae in the west. These sites are older than the proud pyramids of Egypt.

> *History can tell nothing; not a word or a name comes out of the silence - there are a few ambiguous scratches on a wall at Skara Brae. We wander clueless through immense tracts of time. Imagination stirs about a scattered string of bone beads found in Skara Brae. Did the girl have no time for adornment when a westerly gale choked the doors with sand; or did sea raiders tear them from her neck? . . . The Orkney imagination is haunted by time; it is Edwin Muir's great theme, and in this matter he is the poet who speaks for all of us.*

What will be one of George Mackay Brown's great themes soon emerges: what he sees as the modern worship of progress and technology.

> *There is a new religion, Progress, in which we all devoutly believe, and it is concerned only with material things in the present and in a vague golden-handed future. It is a rootless utilitarian faith, without beauty or mystery; a kind of blind unquestioning belief that men and their material circumstances will go on improving until some kind of nirvana is reached and everyone will be rich, free, fulfilled, well-informed, masterful. Why should Orcadians not believe in Progress? - everything seems to insist on it. The stone cots of their grandfathers, where men and animals bedded down under the same roof, are strewn all about the parishes and islands, beside the smart modern houses of wood and concrete. The horses are banished, but then tractors and lorries are much less trouble, much more efficient. There is no real poverty any more; tramps and vagrants and tinkers are exiled with the horses. (Only the very backward farmers nowadays don't have a car.) Progress is a goddess who, up to now, has looked after her children well. The sky is scored with television aerials. There is a family planning centre. There are drifts of books and oil paintings and gramophone records everywhere. And still the shower of good things intensifies.*
>
> *It is difficult to picture this goddess of plenty other than as some huge computer-figure, that will give our children what they desire easily and endlessly - food, sex, excitement - a synthetic goddess, vast and bland as Buddha, but without love or tenderness or compassion; activated only by a mania to create secondary objects that become increasingly shinier and shoddier and uglier.*
>
> *I feel that this religion is in great part a delusion, and will peter out in the marsh.*

I need to think about this. In fact, another glass of Highland Park is required. Technology has given us this whisky, this CD player, this music, and this house, so well-insulated against the gales and driving rain that hit us full on in this exposed place. Why is this progress, or even Progress, so bad? The lament goes on.

> *A community like Orkney dare not cut itself off from its roots*

*and sources....The goddess exacts tribute in subtle ways. For example: there is a kind of shame nowadays in using the old words. And Orkney, only a generation ago, abounded in characters, surrealist folk walked our roads and streets, Dickensian figures with earth and salt in them. Nowadays there is a distinct trimming and levelling-up; a man is ashamed to be different from his neighbour. The old stories have vanished with the horses and the tinkers; instead of the yarn at the pier-head or the pub, you are increasingly troubled with bores who insist on telling you what they think....and you may be sure it isn't their own thought-out opinion at all, but some discussion they have heard on TV the night before, or read in the Daily Express - and now, having chewed it over, they must regurgitate it for you.*

*Word and name are drained of their ancient power. Number, statistic, graph are everything.*

*We have come a long way in a few years.*

Well. Stories and language are this man's passion. His writing is elegant, but is he not mentally and emotionally embedded in some mythical "golden age"? Or is he a prophet who is naming our losses at a time when we are becoming captive to the gee-gaws from a technological cornucopia which is making us delusional? What is this Orkney poet's agenda?

*It is a word, blossoming as legend, poem, story, secret, that holds a community together and gives a meaning to its life. If words become functional ciphers merely, as they are in white papers and business letters, they lose their 'ghosts' - the rich aura that has grown about them from the start, and grows infinitesimally richer every time they are spoken. They lose more; they lose their `kernel', the sheer sensuous relish of utterance. Poetry is a fine interpretation of ghost and kernel. We are in danger of contenting ourselves with husks...I will attempt to get back to the roots and sources of the community, from which it draws its continuing life, from which it cuts itself off at its peril. With the help of the old stories, the old scrolls, the gathered legends, and the individual earth-rooted imagination, I will try to discover a line or two of the ancient life-giving heraldry.*

Questions pile up. Is this a futile railing against modern trends which have manifestly improved the quality of life of many people? Is George Mackay Brown, as some critics have suggested, a provincial writer with a small-town mentality? Brown is undoubtedly an exceptional wordsmith who understands himself as having a spiritual, almost monk-like, vocation; but is this kind of calling past its philosophically credible sell-by date for people living in the 21st century? Questions such as these will emerge as we follow the spiritual journey of a complex and gifted writer who rarely left the island archipelago of his birth, yet who has a growing international reputation. But first, in order to provide a necessary personal context for this exploration, I must digress in order to talk about a different journey.

It is December 9$^{th}$, 1990. We – my wife, two of our three children, one decrepit Labrador, one hamster and myself – have left our friends' house in Nethybridge, Highland Scotland, not much after six in the morning in a virtual white-out. The car radio keeps telling us that motorists shouldn't be going out in this winter blizzard unless they absolutely have to. Well, we have to. Further up the road a removal van, packed with our worldly goods from Glasgow, is ploughing through the snows. Destination, Orkney. The drive plays havoc with the nerve-endings, but after an eternity in a steamed-up Ford Escort, the port of Scrabster suddenly appears. O blessed Scrabster! Soon we are crossing the Pentland Firth, notorious for the turbulence of its two colliding tides. Today, though, the sea is calm. Unlike our previous two trips, we don't have to lie down on the St Ola ferry, feeling unwell. Soon enough, we can see from the boat the faint outlines of Orkney. When we roll off the ferry at Stromness pier, we are rewarded with a breathtaking sight. The ground is white with sparkling frost, the sky a mixture of blues and pink. In the kitchen of a little house in Stromness, a lantern-jawed man has just set aside the lined notebook in which he has been scribbling with a ball-point pen. We turn right in the direction of Orkney's capital, Kirkwall. When we reach the St Magnus Cathedral manse, ready for the unloading of our furniture, a welcoming fire is blazing in the hearth.

We are home, even though we have never before lived in Orkney.

At the watchnight service in a packed St Magnus Cathedral, I hardly know a soul. Looking out from the pulpit, I see up to a thousand people, many of them standing. Believers, semi-detached believers and non-believers, they have spilled from homes and pubs and parties. What are they looking for? A few are there to check out the new St Magnus minister from the urban south. At least that's their cover story. Some who hang on by their fingernails to improbable ledges of faith may be looking for a word of reassurance. There will be those who, under the cover of jocularity, secretly hope that something of the eternal will slip in under their defences and whisper an intimation of immortal love. In the safety of the crowd, they will mouth half-remembered Christmas songs, some full of sentiment and dubious theology. (The little Lord Jesus, like all well-behaved Victorian children, apparently no crying did make). As whisky fumes and yearning fill the air, memories will come flooding back – of school carol services, of punches traded with siblings as presents were unwrapped, of more innocent times, of family life fractured by divorce or bereavement. Tears will roll down cheeks. At midnight, as the lights of the Cathedral are dimmed and the choir sing *Still the Night,* there will be those who unexpectedly experience a striking of the hour of grace, a word-become-flesh in the mysterious cradle of the heart.

I welcome people to the Cathedral. It seems almost impertinent to do so, because I've only been in Orkney five minutes and this is *their* Cathedral. The beautiful, yet simple, red and yellow sandstone Viking temple doesn't belong to any one church, but to the people of Orkney. When I think of the long line of bishops and priests and ministers since the Cathedral's founding in 1137, I'm aware that my time here, however short or long, will be a miniscule part of that historical record. Having been a community minister in the huge Glasgow housing scheme of Easterhouse, and leader of the ecumenical Iona Community, this is my first attempt at parish ministry. I am nervous about it. I wonder about the expectations of this big congregation on this special night, and whether I will be able to meet them. Indeed whether I *should* try to meet them. There are skulls and skeletons along the walls of the ancient church, reminders of mortality. As if I need them after a recent serious health scare. And my own faith? Will the hushed congregation want me to believe *for* them? Can I even believe for myself? Probably, yes, with a bit of help from the poets. Maybe even from the bard of Stromness? Perhaps with a temporary suspension of doubt, most of us will be captivated this night by the fabulous language of Bethlehem, about a peasant girl, a hidden Madonna, pregnant with hope, in a cattle shed because there is no place at the inn. As the man from Hamnavoe (the Stromness of Mackay Brown's imagination) has written in his notebook:

*From a pub door here and there*
*A random ribald song*
*Leaks on the air.*

*The innkeeper over the fire*
*Counting his haul, hears not*
*The cry from the byre.*
*But rummaging in the till*
*Grumbles at the drunken shepherds*
*Dancing on the hill;*

*And wonders, pale and grudging,*
*If the strange pair below*
*Will pay their lodging.*

(*From *The Lodging*, CP p 28)

(Extracts from *An Orkney Tapestry*, George Mackay Brown; Victor Gollancz, London, 1969)

## Kate Barrett

# Home to Roost

I watched the starlings as you lay,
Veer and wheel and wheel again,
Divide and gather in their flocks
Against the dimming sky.
Hundreds guided by their love
Of freedom, space and joy,
And as they changed and sped and flew,
I knew
That our amorphous past
And our tomorrows were the same -
How our joint lives had turned as well.
We'd lost but come together through
Your pain.
And as the light left soft the sky
I saw your eyes fade too, and die.

# Ragnhild Ljosland

## Let the Soul Fly

Candle in the window lit
Hold on, don't go yet
Orange - chilly draft - then black

## New

I am new
Here
Pittan new soonds i me mooth
I even hiv a new nem
Cuz no-one here can pronounce me
auld one
Me gear cam in a container across the
sea
But A'm left the auld me
Ahint
Wae me bruck
An no-one kens who
I was
But aal ken who
I am noo
I am new
I am new noo

## Yvonne Gray

### Leaving

So soon the air grows cold
and the dark draws in.
Across grey sky skeins of geese
drift in gabbling waves.
But today the sea is blue, blue
as it floods from the horizon
and fills your eyes
and your heart is caught

snagged
by that small red boat that gleams
in the low sunlight, poised
on calm water
a fisherman hauling creels
off Braga.

# Christie Williamson

## Arc

I juggle boats
for my oldest son.
He throws them

from his bath.
I catch them,
use their gunwales

as Meridia,
send them sailing
through the air.

Sometimes they stay
up there as long
as it takes

for the present
to slip
into the past.

Oliver laughs.
I remember
when someone else

was the clown
wishing that he
was the child again.

# Mead

Hit scunnirs me at sumeen
could come sa faur an try sa herd
an dø sa weel an persevere
an keep his bow abön da waves
an bail an row an sail an steer
an eftir aa da swaet an spray
ir sokt him clean a wrang ideas
tae see him come sa closs an still
hae nae fent glimpse on his horizon
ta point himsel at, ta inspire him
dan yit he fins athin his hert
nae idder mead'll keep him gjaain
an even if he dusna keen fir sure he'll ivver win
da ony pliss he'd ivver keen ta want ta try ta be
is hem.

## Tessa Ransford

# Gravity and Grace: Arctic Terns at Balnakil

Arctic rhapsodist from Celestial North
or stellar emanation at speed of light
  a dancing wheel around *Polaris*
    *Dubhe, Arcturus,* the great, the dark one

Flier in diagonal cruciform
on angled tapering wing with festooning plumes
  indented tail your daring signal
    mackerel clouds as your chariot-bearers

Come wind come storm come darkness come Great White Bear
our navigation  sure, our direction set
  from Callanish the pillars point us
    upward and northward beyond our knowledge

And every step we tread on our stony ground
reveals the elemental, the fiery pull
  from airy sky to waterlilies
    arc of your flight to translucent petal

Black your diving head into white sea spray
with blood-red beak as you rise and soar away
  like Orphic music you transpose us
    where the horizon turns earth to heaven

# Touchstone

warm
cold
quick
dead
crone
bride
the arch priestess

sharp
pleated
sloped
straight
strong
grounded
the ruler upright

sea
shore
cave
contour
high
low
the far alignment

awake for spring
dawn and colour
for sun and moon
long wake of winter

wheel of shadows
weave of stars
and eyelids close
at crimsoned dusk

For Cairnholy standing stones, Galloway, Equinox 2009

# Amy Allan

## Warmth, Constricted

Ticking clocks and keys in locks,
Lentil soup, and lavender.
Antique plates and pristine gates,
Obligations on the calendar.

Games of cards and being on guard,
Handfuls of pennies to win.
Tarts to bake and pride to take,
Wash your hands, begin.

Treats to guzzle, familial puzzles,
Plenty of space to run.
Just do it where they're not aware
You're having so much fun.

Personal histories lie in mystery,
Textbooks recounted instead.
Better to ask of tomorrow's task,
As you're cosy and snug in your bed.

*

From this distance I find (in a bit of a bind)
That the impact of love can be warming.
I want to have thrown from this place I had grown
A sense of myself, conforming.

In their wake the structure has crumbled a little,
We build as we feel we are able.
But I fear I cannot undo years of "Do not"
And lick knives and leave elbows on tables.

## Doreen Sinclair

### Bird seasons

Spring's boisterous wind
sets rooks aloft
and blackbirds to the song.

A summer's day,
a breath of flowers,
the lift of skylark sounds.

Low flying leaves
and swallows turn
to autumn's starling swirls.

Ice shards send their
winter arrows in
the skein of wild goose calls.

### Home

wraps its warm arms
around
the smell of pancakes
and polish.
My mother's smell
when she was young
and we were children.

# Leaving

LONG-TAILED DUCKS

## Sylvia Hays

# Leaving

Leaving the cold, the damp, the mould
where lime never left the edge of my teeth or my lungs,
leaving the boat hauled up behind the house
("That's wir fether's yole," said the grandfather to all who asked) -
I pack, for the next return, those things to be saved from damp's destruction
clean ash from the grate, store coal and dross, and
close the door on the joy
of improvising a life from the riches of poverty.
I turn the key, rusty and unaccustomed to being turned,
put that, too, in its hiding place
with a valedictory grief as if I were
never coming back:
all in the dark this was done.

Then: morning would just be breaking over the Ola's deck, the sun
rising and forcing gold through cloud -
one more layer of heartbreak,
to sail past Hoy into the open sea,
to point in the wrong direction, South,
away from that place imprinted on me as surely as on any gosling,
that place I understood as home
where I could lie on the ground and
align myself to the points of the compass:
North, to the Merry Dancers,
South to the skerries' lighthouse flashing its beam on my chimney,
East and West to the ancient tomb,
to the entrance to Scapa Flow,
that one place where I could understand where I am,
where I could connect
my small, unregarded, unseen, unwritten life to
the charted world of the compass, to the greater universe
of constellations and black holes and feel that
I am in it and it is in me.

# Fran Flett Hollinrake

## Caritas

Extract from a Novel in progress

When her mother died, Olivia felt nothing but relief. She had played the part of the youngest daughter diligently, and followed her parents' Victorian notions of duty by staying at home to look after them in their old age. Her sisters had both married and now lived too far away to be of any use.

Her mother's death left Olivia financially independent (her reward for giving up her youth, she supposed) and she was at liberty to pursue whatever dream had not been stifled by the claustrophobia of the sickroom. Lying on her wooden bed and hearing the springs creak beneath her, Olivia's first thought was 'away'. Away to where, though? She had never travelled and had little curiosity to see the world. If she had a companion perhaps, or a husband, then a journey of exploration might have been undertaken, but at the age of thirty-two Olivia could not envisage herself mounting camels, or taking a train across continents. She could not see the point of holidays.

What leisure time Olivia had enjoyed during her parents' years of dotage had been spent in self-education. She had forced herself through her father's leather-bound Classics (mostly untouched by him and some with pages still uncut); and to stretch her mind through the long nights of nursing, had taught herself German in order to study the works of the great German philosophers. Her sisters, in their rare visits, had accused her of being humourless. They'd be bloody humourless, she thought, if they had to wipe the ancient backsides.

Olivia's glance drifted around her book-stuffed room and she allowed her mind to slip. Heidegger and Kierkegaard sat alongside Milton and Keats. A collection of dog-eared Bibles paid testament to Olivia's early religious leanings, borne out of years of her father's stern voice and the silent, dusty Sundays. From her prone position, she stretched out her hand and slid her bedside Bible onto her chest and opened it at random, just in case it yielded any words of wisdom. It didn't. It offered her a page of begats, doing no more than reminding her of her loveless state of spinsterhood.

Her first task was to clear out her parents' belongings and clean the house from top to bottom. The scrubbing of the sickroom floor provided a monotonous rhythm to Olivia's thoughts: 'What shall I do? What shall I do? What shall I do?' she muttered under her breath. It never occurred to Olivia to do nothing: it was simply not in her nature. She heaped musty coats and flat, mouldy leather brogues onto the cart of the rag-and-bone man and locked her father's Great War medals in her keepsake box. As she swept out her mother's wardrobe, she found a pile of old school exercise books, inscribed with her own fastidious hand. Untying the string she was faced with faded ink lines of Latin and Greek and the reminder that she had once shown an aptitude for scholarship. Her hand paused in the turning of the pages.

A fortnight later a brown envelope arrived bearing pamphlets and booklets. A month after that, a letter, bearing a florid embossed crest, informed Olivia that if the financial arrangements were found to be in order, her place at the Faculty of Theology in Paderborn, Westphalia, Germany, would be secured.

---

Olivia looked up from her papers. The wooden sash window rattled in its frame and outside a rook flew from one pinnacle to another. A blast of air rushed down the chimney and sent a plume of ash and smoke into Olivia's room. She chewed the end of her pen and surveyed the mass of books and papers and ink on her desk – what time was it? Indeed, what day was it? Had she eaten? Casting around for clues she saw a paper bag from a nearby bakery, but judging from the layer of dust on it, she concluded that it had been there for some time.

She stood up, arched her back and stretched, her joints cracking. The window rattled again and looking out, she saw a swirl of leaves eddying around the courtyard. There was no-one about, but then she wasn't looking for anyone – her days here were mostly untroubled by human contact. Every now and again she sought out the silent old woman who looked after her rooms, gave her a five-mark note and asked her to get toiletries and food – nothing fancy – Olivia's taste buds had long been dulled by invalid fare. A bag of bread, sausage, ground coffee and occasionally apples, would appear silently at her door, along with the coins, which were stacked up neatly in order of size. On her single gas ring she brewed coffee and drank it thick and dark – her one vice, she would say to herself.

Every month or so Olivia climbed the broad stone steps to the college department where Herr Professor Schmidt held court. The Professor always looked surprised to see her, but once she had drawn forth the handful of notes and papers from her leather satchel (once her father's), he was happy to discuss her work and ideas. Sometimes he would reach into the dark varnished cupboard and take out a bottle of sherry and two sticky glasses, and they would sit, one either side of the fireplace, talking until the college housekeeper came to turn down the lamps. She felt happiest there – if the satisfaction of philosophical grappling and a sense of not wanting to be anywhere else could be described as happiness. The feeling lasted until she got back to her own room, heated up the dregs of the morning's coffee and climbed under her quilt for warmth. Using a pile of books as a bedside table, she would read for hours, thinking about life in the abstract and sometimes hearing her sisters' voices of pity. They had both sent letters over the last year, but Olivia had stopped opening them after a while – they seemed to have nothing to say except things of a domestic nature – children, garden, troublesome housemaids. Two or three unopened envelopes lay strewn under her desk.

As she watched the leaves being stripped of their foliage, Olivia decided that perhaps it was time to go home for a visit. There were documents and things to do with her parents' house that she had to attend to, and she supposed she should visit her growing and uninteresting collection of nephews and nieces. Wrapping herself in a thick woollen coat (her mother's best and too good to throw out) and pulling on gumboots, she headed down the street to the railway station. How much was a passage back to Britain? She couldn't remember how much it had cost to get here – she just knew that you could get a single ticket at the station that got you from one place to another.

The streets were quiet, but it was still early morning, she realised. What if the station didn't open until later? The wooden gate creaked and she saw the smoke from the Bahnhof guard's pipe through the hatchway. Relieved, Olivia pulled off her mittens and in her crisp, clear voice asked for a passage to London. The station guard took his pipe from his lips and gave her a strange look. She repeated her request.

'London. In England,' she said again.

He smiled and leaned forward.

'Fraulein, it is not possible to go to England' he said.

'Whyever not? Is there a problem with the train?' she frowned. This was most inconvenient.

'No, Fraulein. You cannot go to England because we are at war with England'.

---

It was snowing hard. The line of people stamped their feet and blew on their fingers as they waited for the office to open. The internment office was manned by a retired policeman who had been hoping to spend his retirement doing nothing more than growing cabbages. In the few conversations she had had with him, Olivia had gleaned that working for the Reich was not a matter of choice; he had confided in her that his daughter was hoping to get a secretarial position, and that by co-operating he would smooth the path for her. It would not do, the daughter had said, for her father to show unwilling.

Herr Brocken unlocked the iron gate and they filed in. Looking around, Olivia saw the French teacher, Pierre. He nodded at her – he was here most mornings. At the front of the queue to have her papers checked she saw Frau Weiss, an American who had married a German musician shortly before the war. Whilst he travelled Europe playing to the troops, his wife was under strict controls. America might be a neutral country, but the talk was that they would swing the Allies' way if push came to shove.

Herr ex-Polizei looked at her papers and slid the forms under the glass for her to sign.

'Cold today.' It was a statement of fact, rather than a question.

'Yes,' she said. Then, thinking this might be her only social interaction of the day, she made herself speak.

'Is the butcher's open today, do you know?' she said, pushing the papers back. Her voice sounded cracked and croaky.

'Oh yes,' he looked up, his forehead catching the orange glow of the streetlight. 'Herr Jonathan came in last night with some good meat. You should go quick!' His eyes flickered at the queue behind Olivia and he leaned forward, baring his yellow teeth.

'Your friend Herr Jonathan will save the best bits for the English

Fraulein, eh?' he laughed and looked delighted at his own wit. Olivia made herself smile and left the office quickly.

Outside, in the street the snow was still swirling, coating the drab streets with a layer of white. There was already a queue at the butcher's. Herr Brocken was right – there had clearly been a delivery. A tired-looking woman with yellow hair came out, clutching a seeping brown parcel. She scowled at Olivia, who lowered her gaze; she should be used to it by now – the underlying resentment towards an enemy foreign national. It would be no consolation to the woman to know that Olivia's movements were severely restricted, and that she was obliged to report to the authorities every day. As far as the local *volk* were concerned, she was a snake in their midst – a snake fed and clothed at their expense, eating food that they could be giving to their children.

At the butcher's counter she peered through the smeared glass. A plate of glistening offal seemed the freshest thing on offer. There was no indication of what animal it had once been, but Olivia swallowed hard and bought a kilo. Lowering her head against the battering wind and snow, she walked the two miles back to the convent. She pulled the iron ring and heard the bell ring deep inside the medieval walls. Sister Konstanza peered through the bars, saw who it was, and hefted the circle of keys hanging at her belt.

Olivia walked to her cell, removed her sodden coat, and took the parcel of meat to the convent kitchen. She pulled a bucket of small grey potatoes towards her and began to peel.

Note: Caritas is Latin for charity.

# Poems written in Writing Workshops at Westray Junior High School, May 2010

## Emily Jones
### Barmouth

Lying on the beach
It's extremely hot out here
There's a slight breeze blowing my hair
From my shoulder to my back

I'm lying down on my towel
The corner keeps on blowing over my feet
The sand is smooth
And the crabs are on the shore

The seagulls swoop down as I drop a sandwich by accident
I can feel my shoulders burning
I put some sun cream on
The sand sticks to me as I walk to the sea

I pick up a crab and it nips my finger
I lay it down on the sand and it scuttles away
I say goodbye and it's gone
The wave hits my toes and it's quite cold

## Sophie Sumner
### Colchester Zoo

I can't stand the heat anymore,
We're on the way to Colchester Zoo,
I can't wait!
I'm sitting with my niece in the back of the car,
Playing with her all the time,
She falls asleep,
Snoring quietly she wriggles around,
My goodness, she is beautiful,
With one hand clutching her little pink cup,
Her little head resting on the other.

## Solan Dodman
### Corsica

Laying in the sea
spreading my legs out
letting the waves push me
into the shore
then diving into the currents
and feeling my hair in the waves
and doing it over
and over again.

## Shane Hourston
### County Show

At the County Show
Sun is out
Just a warm breeze

Noise fills the air
Stalls and rides
Smell of food

Fun
Happy
With family

## Callum Booth
### Manchester

Wet rainy concrete
MP3 Player, my mind pretending ease
dark thoughts (you know, thugs and knives)
mud and smashed glass beneath my feet.
I hear voices, footsteps
must be the weather whistling
I see a glint from the corner of my eye
I see the mud and smashed glass beneath me.

## Rowan Pierce
### Liza Beck

Hazy hills show rain drenched clouds
Beyond the valley folds,
Swathed in scraggly heather,
Cloaked in air that's icy cold.

Tumbling over the pounded rocks,
A beck as clear as a watery mirror,
Frosty stalactite daggers wait;
Icicles draped like chandeliers.

The gnarled oak leans with the wind
Towards the plummeting flow,
Banishing the landscape's faults
And sweeping them far below.

Crisp winter air moulds over the hills,
As weather-beaten herdwicks watch over
The landscape which formed their features
The weather-weary Lake District rovers.

## Stefan Muir
### Portugal

waves crashing
blowing fresh air on my face
the sun wafting heat
melting sinking into the sea
waiting on the other side
the moon shines on the water.

## Marianne Wood
## The Aberdeen Day

Contented on the beach with the old rotten fences
Innocent warmth reflects on my back
I lie in the sun, losing the will to my senses
The length of my energy is far too lack

The waves lap up against the sand
The birds annoy us up in the sky
I grab some stones with my hand
And throw them across making them go high

The gulls go to feed their screeching chicks
I walk away home along with my friend
The calm sea just laps and licks
And the sunset day comes to a beautiful end.

## Molly Bradley
## The Unicorn

She stands there,
Waiting,
Hoping,
For her child to come home

A bush shakes
From side to side
Like a soft breeze
Has come over it

A glimpse
Of pure white
Comes through the bush
It's her child

A glimpse of sharp,
Hideous teeth make her jump
That is no child of hers

White leopard
From the north
Her child between his teeth

# Between Twilight and Night*

PURPLE SANDPIPERS

*From *George Mackay Brown: The Wound and the Gift* by Ron Ferguson

## Morag MacInnes

# A Scottish novel

You sup it up don't you, the brose of it.
How he hit the highroad, mother in a mutch is it? -
at the ben end, under the rowan, shouting don't forget the spurtle.
Drink them hardy hurdies down, that meal bag bursting
on his peat hill shoulder. Snoosh him in,
he's ramping Reekwards as you read,
Donald, Ranald, Allan, Callum, in a skirt. With a
dirk.

Licky licky, awful sticky, that coo candy.
Poor but right passionate, under the blue
and the painted mountains, Walter's lad o
pairts. Breathe in the steam of him
ploshing a stream in the brackeny fairnteckle glen. Awesome and awe full,
the antlers,
the fish birling uphill in wilderness. Oh!

But beware, that's
tame fare - just you
compare noo.
Gardieloo!

Here's hussies in howffs, deils and anatomists waiting to
pounce on the douce. Murdo and Hector, dogging around
in a clapshot of psalmsong and sex in a boxbed. What with
the debtors, the dice and delirium – mammie's
meal's in the press,
mouldering. The spurtle's grown a thistle
head. It's cock a leekie time. Petticoat tails. Rich pickings in middens,
for magpies
and rats. Fill up a poke of them!

Boiled through, spiced up, string loosed, how will
the clootie dumpling slice? Might he
make money ground from dirt he named for home, build palaces,
be painter to the nabob? Die fenced, with angels, having sent his shares
in sealing waxy parcels to Drumsheugh?
Or, kiltie cauld bum on the Baltic sea, leave not a crumb
for you to feast upon? There'll be
a genteel tussle for his final slice, but have no fear.
There's aye a bap in the oven.

# On being asked whether Orcadians still told stories

Because spit and there's a body
doesna
buy a round/share the booty/wrap a raffle

some puir chiel
wi a leg/keek/granny/coo
no quite right

because there's aye a sowl
kens it all/shouts the odds/spills the beans

aye a bird and a worm and a cow
in a market

or a lass
on a task
for a master/for a troll/for a meal

because the closes reel
wi fellas on the strut
pulling stunts/pulling stepmas/pulling legs

because there's wives wi webs
o mince/ten gallon boots/red riding hoods

how could there no be
aye
a teller/mindan on/takkan aff/passan time
aye
a listener/on a break/wi a drink/in the bus
aye a tale.

# Kirsty Macdonald

## The Unseen Tide

The cousins met in the old house, just as they had done years ago. They were taller, heavier and better-dressed now, with the lines of the years beginning to congregate at corners of eyes and mouths. But the subtleties of their smiles hadn't changed at all since those days of childhood summers.

Between them sat a bottle of vodka, all the way from Russia – after all, you can't have a reunion of this type without a small something to aid the flow of nostalgia. It glugged as it poured and filled the glasses of memory with a pleasing, familiar sound.

Despite their shared beginnings their lives had diverged enough to disallow any glibness in this meeting – work needed to be done to uncover old common ground. John had stayed on the island and was a fisherman; James had headed south years before and was now a financial adviser in the city, earning 30 a year plus bonuses, or so he tried to tell his younger cousin with pride. John wasn't sure what he meant – a bonus to him was catching enough in a week to be able to pay all his bills and have a little something left over to enjoy in the hotel. Sometimes he even cut out the middle man and kept a few small lobsters and a couple of mackerel back to give to Davey behind the bar in exchange for an evening's tab. Those were good nights.

James listened quietly and politely, there in the kitchen of the house where their fathers had grown up, and stood, laughed and argued together. The tales of nights in the bar, with the same stock characters and always the same outcomes made him mildly uncomfortable, like sitting in a smoky room with a too-low ceiling. Strange to him now, this small life that was all so familiar and used to contain an entire universe, from the rock pools where they'd fished as boys to the dance hall where they'd spied on girls years later. He loosened his tie and tried to follow John's story of the very rare sun-fish he'd seen from the boat last week, the first one he'd seen in thirteen years. But James's mind migrated back to his real life, arriving at the seafood restaurant he'd taken Vanessa to last month with a view to finally proposing. Was sun-fish on the menu that night? Most things that money can buy were, rare or not. It was an impressive yet understated 1 carat, the diamond in the ring in the blue velvet box that remained firmly in his pocket after she'd informed him she'd decided to take the job in London, and would be leaving next week. They had parted like clients after a meeting, shaking hands.

He'd dropped it in the firth on his way home. Maybe the tides had carried it all the way here. Something like an unseen tide had surely carried him back.

As in times past, they decided a walk down the shore in the dying light of the summer night might help to clear heads. John was aware he'd lost his cousin during his stories, but had put it down to the fact that Jamie probably couldn't hold his drink these days. It was a well-known fact that if you moved south you lost your drinking skills. They left the building, door ajar and lit up like a lighthouse, and walked towards the smell of brine and the sound of waves. A few minutes in, however, another smell entirely hit their nostrils like a brick in the face. 'What the hell is that?!' screamed James.

'Oh come on Jamie, dinna tell me you've forgotten the most memorable perfume of them all?' John replied, the old diminutive name of childhood beginning again to sit more comfortably with his cousin. 'It's a dead whale, man. Been there twa-three weeks. You'd stink too if you'd been lying dead on a beach that long.' At that the two giggled like schoolboy companions again, and hurried on to investigate with an old familiar feeling of adventure.

And there it was, easily twenty feet long, bird-pecked and beginning to fester, but quite recognisably a dead Minke. 'It's a Minke', Jamie thought aloud.

'See, you haven't lost all yer skills in the soft south. Here's the real test though, is it male or female?' His eyes twinkled with mirth at the challenge laid down to his old friend. Remembering full well that only the males venture into the colder Northern waters, Jamie saw his window and replied, 'I dunno, let's take down its breeks and find out.' The two men laughed, together.

Once they'd calmed themselves, brought back quickly by the stomach-churning stench as the wind changed direction, John paced the whale's length. 'Twenty-two feet, mind that on will you Jamie man. I'll need to phone this in in the morning.'

'Whit for man? It's surely just a tasty treat for the gulls? Nature'll do its work and the thing'll be gone soon enough.'

'Sure indeed, but they're officially "toxic waste" these days, and I don't want any creatures, human or otherwise, getting ill. They keep all their toxins in the fat just under their skin, you know. All the crap we pump into the sea, soaked up and stored right there in their blubber. It won't be hunting by our Scandinavian brothers that'll put paid to these beasts, but something much more passive. Makes you think.'

Jamie nodded, looking like a dog that had just been shown a card trick. It had made him think, bewildered and eventually shocked him. He'd later remember with some guilt all the trans-Atlantic flights he'd taken, all the plastic involved in his lifestyle, and the cruise to the Arctic that he and Vanessa had been on last summer.

The two stared at the animal for a while, taking in its size and alien form. 'Come on, let's head back – that vodka's getting warm', said John, grinning. Jamie took one last walk round the whale, and noticed something small and blue lying just by its head. It was a box. He picked it up and opened it: empty now, a blue velvet box that had once contained something valuable. Smiling to himself, he threw it over his shoulder, returning it to its toxic keeper, and trotted up the dune to join his companion.

## Alistair Peebles

# And So

It starts again with cutting ground,
turf peeled back and soil turned,
on a February morning, bright,
*for a wonder*, and warm.

The blades mirror a dark earth,
well-kent, it seems, and kind,
for scarce a stone drags out
to snag or blunt them,

sheer forms, heirlooms often,
hauled inch-fine by experts, all
on their mettle at the Match today,
at Vola, Grimeston, Harray.

In ploughing time, generations gone,
strips uncoil between beast and man,
or now, between a man
and the beasts to come after.

Lonely, sometimes, up in the cab –
*a public office for one* – but here's
company, competition, cups of tea,
and prizes, a write-up, a yarn...

'Vola'? from 'vole'? I'm wondering,
remembering earlier, at the loch,
when I'd parked in a freezing fog,
and trailed among the standing stones

and over the bitten grass so lately
slabbed with ice, and over the tunnels
the voles had made, a network
like veins, discovered by the thaw.

I'd been thinking of a friend,
the photographs she'd taken there,
of myself taking photographs now
and then her man came to mind

who'd been telling me, this winter,
walking – *oh, it helps* – into town,
he'd heard them under the snow,
squeaking and scratching...

You can't be sure, of course, where
any of this is going, day by day,
but then a day comes round
when an hour after standing

by the frozen loch, chilling,
thinking of friends, admiring voles,
watching swans drift back and forth
in their own clear path, you find yourself

for *it's turned out fine*, in shirtsleeves,
tractors tilting over the old ground;
a vapour, breath-like, sunlit for a moment,
there, above the loam.

# Alison Flett

## 6 Cycling Poems

### shed

getting the bike out
the hardest bit – so tangled
with all the other stuff

### focus

fields hills buildings - blurred
only the road ahead
clear and constant

### hill

thighs aching
I switch to a lower gear,
keep climbing

### peak

at the crest of the last hill
I realise
it was the second last

### breath

cycling back from the cemetery
lungs pumping
heart pounding

### descent

free-wheeling all the way
catching flies in my teeth

## Bill Ferguson

# The Effing Pips

it's six o'clock on friday the thirtieth of whenever    good morning    it's been giving him the pip for months so while the would-be author sits scratching his head and tinkering round the edges of the dilemma he's faced with he thinks he'll just check how things are sounding news- and weather-wise on the beeb before getting down to some serious displacement activity so stubs out his cigarette and drains the dregs from his second mug of tea at the same time as he's hearing first estimates of whether the economy grew in the first three munfs *pip!* of the year will be published later today by the office for national statistics our economics editor stephanie flanders reports says our newsreader this morning neil sleet with no perceptible pause but with a smattering of ahrs and tee-aitches whereupon with perfect equanimity and without further ado today the oh en ess will offer its first guess about national output during the first three munfs *pip!* of the year says stephanie the beeb's borderline scary frontline authority on esoteric matters such as munf-on-munf trends who like most city experts expects modest groaf *pip!* of around nought point four percent in line with the groaf-rate *pip!* in the previous quarter when the ewe kay finally pulled out of recession she's explaining with a couple of rare reassuring ahrs plus an audible flare of one nostril while mid slurp of his fird mug of tea the would-be author is offering his first guess about the notional input of the fird of the first free phantom full stops of neil and steph's combined contributions during the previous firty-free seconds an ill-judged estimate as it transpires since it seems the bad weather in january hit large parts of the economy continues steph in the interests of clarity and completeness and so forf so as well as necessitating a furver outbreak of clauses today's estimate relies heavily on data collected in the first two munfs *pip!* of the year at which point the would-be aufor seems to have lost track of the edges he was tinkering with so resorts to brewing a fourf mug of tea and rolling himself an eightf cigarette whilst finking about metaphor and metonymy and all manner of year-on-year notional national patois-groaf trends until It's Six Minutes Past Six    Philip!    The Weather    is it gunna get warmer? demands mister humphrys who's got no truck wif notional or national meteorological niceties cus he's The Man and you don't mess wiv him even on a good day   john   sara(h)   gooood morning! responds philip who has a way of sounding alarmingly upbeat and ready to do somefing impetuous twenty-four seven whatever the wevver but at least we've been spared the likes of lefargic laura and lefal liam and most of all despwerate daniel who must be somewhere else on the airwaves performing his radio-unfriendly taekwondo-cum-salsa routines the lengf and bwedf of the nation's wevver charts so like   john sara(h) and those of you out and about prettymuch anywhere souf *pip!* of the pennines won't need to wrap up warm in the winter woollies phanks to the ridge of high pressure about which philip's enphusing though   be warned!   it might just be wurf *pip!* taking your brollies to be on the safe side but to get to the details we'll start wif *pip!* wales the west country the whole of the souf *pip!* the midlands east anglia the norf-west *pip!* the norf-east *pip!* including coastal areas where it's going to be a fine day by and large feeling pleasantly warm wif *pip!* long spells of sunshine giving highs of sixteen seventeen degrees around the coast and   hang on to your sombreros!   eighteen possible inland now as we move into norvern *pip!* ireland we've got a scattering of some quite persistent showers to start the day but these should drive froo *pip!* quite quickly on the brisk souf-westerly *pip!* bweeze and fizzle out by mid morning whereupon peppered wiv a preponderance of perishing pips the would-be aufor pops the kettle on forfwif for his fiftf mug of tea effectively effacing a pwoliferation of persevering wegions plus a plefora of persisting compass points wiv the wumble of water as it's weaching the boil along wiv his effing pipometer then nips to the toilet to welieve his bladder while his teabag's infusing weappeawing just in time to catch somefing he's missed is going to be moving into all parts in the course of the day except the far norf *pip!* and that's your wevver for today back to you john thanks philip the Time now is nine minuTes pasT six the greek governmenT says sara(h) wiv or wivout an aspirate aitch who's parTicular abouT enunciaTing her Tees is coming under increasing pwessure over the sTaTe of iTs finances and while ee ewe officials and their eye em eff counTerparTs are as we know working on a possible bail-ouT package greek public secTor worker unions whose members have already Taken To the sTreeTs in recenT weeks To proTesT againsT cuTs in pay and pensions are calling for a one-day national sTrike nexT week well malcolm brabanT our affens *pip!* correspondenT has been following evenTs in the gweek capiTal and joins us on the line now and malcolm presumably the unions are concerned thaT iT will be their members who will have To bear the brunT of the evermore sTringent measures the governmenT inTends To inTroduce in order To comply wif *pip!* the pwe-conditions in any ee ewe bail-ouT plan yes saywa(h) there's gwate concern here in affens *pip!* over the stwictures inherent in any pwoposed combined ee ewe eye em eff bail-out says malcolm our ubiquitous man on the gwound partly as you say because public service workers feel they will be the ones hit hardest by the cuts when the deal goes ahead but partly too because there's widespwead suspicion that the hole in the gweek finances is much larger than had been pweviously fought *pip!* and when you speak to virtually anyone in the stweets of affens *pip!* you're left wiv *pip!* the unmistakable impwession most ordinary gweeks are mightily aggwieved about the pwospect of being landed wiv *pip!* the bill for the unbwidled bwibery and underhand deals and so forf *pip!* which they say are wife in gweek government indeed twust in politicians is so fwagile here at the moment that you'll hear people talk openly about em pees as fieves *pip!* but given the number of well-weported scandals in public affairs in wecent munfs *pip!* this kind of fwaudulent activity is simply the most visible aspect of a blight that many gweeks would claim spweads wight froo *pip!* the gweek public sector as a whole a view pwetty much in line quite fwankly wiv *pip!* those expwessed elsewhere wivin *pip!* the ee ewe that the gweek system is endemically cowwupt and so what wiv all the ensuing discussion about gweece defaulting on its debt wepayments and cwisis talks to shore up the single cuwwency and furver austerity measures aimed at achieving budget cuts of firty billion euwos wiv the goal of weducing gweek public deficit cuwwently standing at firteen point six percent of gee dee pee to less than free percent by two-fousand and fourteen as a pwecondition for any pwoposed ee ewe eye em eff wescue package and so forf it sounds to the would-be aufor as vough the ess aitch eye tee's about to hit the fan big-time an impwession which may or may not be dispelled by stephanie flanders our economics editor who wiv her in-depf knowledge of welf and wecession and wecovery and all the welated wisks to the euwo eye ee as well as of munf-on-munf oh en ess twends and their implications in groaf terms we-joins us here in the studio Oh Phank F'huck it's not wobert peston our business editor wiv anuvver excwuciating ah-ah-ah-littered assault on ig-zzzaCtly H'whadidizzz thut needs to hAPPen in order toooooo to-to-to to get the next word quantitatively eased from his bwain and leveraged out of his mouf so-so-so-so just to keep it simple for listeners John so allOW him to arrIVE ahhhht Thuh absolutelyfundamentalpointinallofthis Sara(h) ovvv'h getting round tooo to-to-to addressing theee thee-thee-thee the m'HASSively importantfiscalresponsibilityofprecipitatingfurverfinancialmeltdown thee-thee-thee would-be aufor's disproportionately exclaiming to himself wiv potentially calamitous consequences for his smoker's cough mid glug of his fiftf mug of tea at the same time as he's wegistering that it's seeming to stephanie actually that some uvver *pip!* fing *pip!* is going on in the gweek situation and that the gweek government doesn't seem to wealise that it has froan *pip!* away its last chance to put its house in order moreover that it's pwetty clear the auforities *pip!* have just not got a handle on this deal at all so since it's twelve minutes past six and it's abundantly clear the would-be aufor's effing pipometer's starting to feel a bit restive again he decides it's time to roll himself another cigarette and just chill while john and sara(h) oversee our first leisurely look at what the newspapers are saying which the would-be aufor misses most of since he's tripped over a fwesh edge to tinker wiv and fallen into a bit of a dwam about how best to tackle what's been bugging him for munfs at the same time as he's wetorically asking himself or asking himself wetorically how many effs not-to-mention vees and double-ewes a morning can cope wiv thus it's a bit ominous to hear the time is quarter past six and nick ravver than adam who so far as the would-be aufor can wecall has good days and bad days as well as so-so days ahrs'n'tee-aitcheswise is here wif the business so wiv everyfing going souf in that world these days it's not looking good but more to the point the would-be aufor's having the customary small wager wiv himself about how long it'll take for groaf and over-the-counter derivatives and synergies of scale going forward etcetwa to make an appearance plus which letter of the alphabet be it ewe vee double-ewe or ell the wecession wesembles on fwiday the firtief of whatever to discuss which our fwiday boss ann(e) wiv a notional ee murphy birdseye's em dee in the ewe kay joins us in the studio good morning says nick good morning says ann(e) you've just published a remarkable set of figures for the last financial year showing profits up a staggering umpteen point free *pip!* percent on the previous year to what do you attribute birdseye's resilience and indeed the continuing groaf *pip!* (nine seconds) of the frozen-food sector as a whole given that the rest of the economy is in deep recession and perhaps more importantly do you fink *pip!* you'll be able to continue to out-perform your competitors going forward (firteen point four seconds) in the event of the double-dip wecession (fourteen point free seconds) that many economists and city analysts are forecasting says nick fankfully wiv helpful intonational punctuation uvverwise we might be inclined to get lost but no not a bit of it ann(e) and her notional ee are confident they'll be very recessionproof once the recession ah pause you know pause moves on plus she's got quite a lot to say about the aforementioned groaf phenomenon suggesting it shows cweditcrunched consumers are retreating to brands they trust and that somefing the would-be aufor failed to catch much to his chagrin it might've been peas is the most pwemium product we've introduced in that area indeed goes so far as to aver that the fact that premium pwoducts are doing so well points to the crucial importance of maintaining brand loyalty which is the lynchpin of the company's strategy going forward (fifty-five seconds) and that her backgwound is very much in branded consumer goods and she's been brought into the company because she's a person who delivers groaf *pip!* and that in real terms she and her notional ee've invested significantly in the business over the last few years but somewhat disappointingly from the would-be aufor's point of view have so far failed to produce much in the way of derivatives or synergies of scale in the preceding seventy-free seconds which is maybe why nick is asking her anuvver question along the lines of how do you respond to the suggestion that what birdseye is doing is irresponsible? in uvver *pip!* words that wif *pip!* so much nervousness around in the financial markets you should be putting a hold on investment especially when companies froo-out *pip!* the ewe kay are cutting costs and levels of investment generally are at an all-time low wiv *pip!* interest-rates at rock bottom and inflation set to rise above free *pip!* percent in the coming munfs *pip!* how given all of the above can you continue to invest at these levels or is a cutback inevitable do you fink? *pip!* not at all protest ann(e) and her notional ee we've done the mafs *pip!* and see huge groaf *pip!* potential for the birdseye brand we're only a few munfs *pip!* into a five-year groaf *pip!* plan moreover we fink *pip!* we've got great groaf *pip!* potential so yes it's a tough decision certainly these calls are never easy to make but frankly wivout *pip!* investment there's no groaf *pip!* ann(e) murphy managing director of birdseye ewe kay many fanks *pip!* intervenes nick in the nick of time before john declares it's twenty-six minutes past six which usually means garry or rob or whoever is here wiv the sport but the would-be aufor's not really noticed which of them it is this morning because his effing pipometer has just hit an all-time high alvough it look as vough it's maybe just beginning to undergo weak wecovery after the london marafon and somefing wiveting about cwicket and somebody or uvver's exciting four-free win last night and fifa's concerns about safety at the fast-appwoaching footie world cup and almost inevitably going forward wiv bareahrs'd effwontewy to the two-fousand and twelve olympics until wiv ineffable efficacy via a summawy of the news followed by somebody or uvver's weview of a weport on unacceptable vawiations in helf or possibly education pwovision nationwide a weport which (to put it mildly) makes for some pwetty dismal weading it has to be said it's twenty-free minutes to seven and the would-be aufor discovers ivor john or sara(h) one or the uvver it couldn't've been boaf has unbeknownst to himself alweady entwusted listeners' auwal wellbeing to our home-affairs cowwespondent whose name has so far eluded him but who is waxing lywical about what a leaked foweign-office memo dwawn up by a junior official duwing a wecent bwainstorming session might portend heaven forfend for the pope's forfcoming state visit and furvermore what cwitics claim said memo weveals about government pwejudice against faif schools whereupon the would-be aufor's effing pipometer suffers double-dip welapse and starts in effect to expewience somefing akin to catastwophic iwwecovewable meltdown of a form which might efficaciously be said to wesemble *pip! pip! pip! pip! pip! pi-pi-pi-pi-pi-piiiiiiiii* wiv a notional aspirate pee at the end of it maybe I should get a life finks the would-be aufor wiv a glance out the window to see what the wevver's doing in the "except" bit of the countwy before wolling himself anuvver cigawette to go along wiv his enf mug of tea then we-tuning to his witer's block

# Mike Hoy

## The Sons of John Barleycorn

Highland is bedecked in Highland dress with a long beard and greying hair, supported by a walking stick. A proud man but with a weary disposition, he seems older than his years.

Speyside wears Highland dress also, but less formal than his elder brother and in newer clothing, fitter and stronger. Knowledgeable and reliable.

Lowland wears tartan trews with a frilled shirt. More of a dandy than the first two, he speaks with a refined accent. Feels slightly ill-at-ease with the family who he feels are coarse and uneducated.

Islay speaks the Gaelic although he can claim to speak the English as a second language. Not in Highland dress but in a fisherman's jumper and corduroy trousers tucked into Wellington boots. A heavily-built man whose strength and power belies his heavy smoking, he doesn't hold back on saying what he feels.

Campbeltown is the oldest of the brothers, wearing faded and threadbare clothing of tweed jacket and gabardine trousers with an ancient waistcoat and battered brogues on his feet. Longs for the days when he and his friends were in their prime and had an enviable reputation.

S – (Standing up and straightening his sporran) How can any of you think you are better than myself to represent this country of ours when I am known and respected throughout the whole world – and England – as the true taste of Scotland? I am what people expect when they come here from foreign lands like the Americas or the Far East.

L – (Laying an empty glass on the table) They may expect to see your shortbread tin image but it's myself that they will stay with. Gone is the romance of Rob Roy MacGregor and Bonnie Prince Charlie.

You have to waken yourself up, man, and drag yourself into the 21st century or you'll end up like Campbeltown's cronies. Gone forever.

C – (Banging his glass on the table and spilling some of his drink) Nonsense, ye impudent young scoundrel! All my cronies are lying in wait and when they return, you will all get a run for your money, especially you, Lowland, wi' your strange accents and fancy clothing – you're just a popinjay! We will reinstate ourselves as the true characters of Scotland, backed up with our rich history. We will lead this country as we did in the past.

I – (Raising his hand to the others) Calm yerself, old man, you don't want to go doing yourself mischief now. We shall talk this thing through like the polite gentlemen we are and not like a rabble of fishwives on the quayside. There is nae doubt that, though we are all faithered by the same man, we all have our own qualities, very different from each other. I myself am more suited to the outdoors and the rugged way of life.

L – (Sneers) That'll be why you smell like a lobster creel that has been buried in peat for years.

I – (Standing up and rolling up his sleeves) I'll gie ye a guid skelp the noo, ma lad.

H – (Raising his voice) Enough. Stop this arguing and behave, the lot o' ye. Wha would think we were all from the same family? Have respect for each other and stop bickering. Islay, it's true that you have the aroma of outside aboot yer person and some see that as a quality that they seek. Myself I'm more diverse than that, and that's what some folk like aboot me. Now we all have something that people want, and together, we can give all those who know us as a family what they seek.

C – I could have done all that in the past wi' all my mates an no' need any o' ye.

H – Aye, ye could have covered most of it, you and yer cronies, but no to the same extent that we as a family can do.

S – Highland is right ye know. Heavens, we've got so many foreigners coming over and trying to take our jobs, and let's face it some of them are damn good at what they do. We have to pool our resources and strengths as a family, get through this invasion and take-over bids.

L – Well, actually I have met quite a few of these foreigners and I must say that most of them are alright. They're not trying to take over; their imitation is more of a respectful acknowledgement of what we are and always will be. Remember that there will never be anyone like us. From Highland Park to Bladnoch, from Glen Garioch to Talisker.

H – Naw, naw ye've got that wrong. There's a new family on my patch now. Abhainn Dearg as Islay will know them, or Red River to the likes o' yerself Lowland. They're out by Uig.

L – Wasn't there a family a long time ago on that site?

H – Aye, no' for 170 years tho', an' they're expecting their first bairns to be with us next year.

S – Och now won't that be grand. It'll be just wonderful to have some youngsters goin' aboot. Ye must introduce them when they arrive.

C – Aye, I can teach them a lot aboot our business.

L – Well as I was saying, from all over Scotland there is no one like us. And we should lead the way. These big guys coming over from abroad are well up to speed with what we are doing but we are still out in front. Alright, some of our cousins in America, like the Bourbon family, are doing very well, but we have the history and if we work together they will never be able to take that away.

I – Ye have a good point there, Lowland. I expect where you bide you are more used to outsiders coming in, but where I am the influx is very seasonal.

C – Aye, very few want to see the islands in the depths of a cold January blast.

S – And that is why we are all who we are. The Scottish weather makes us. Campbeltown, you have a long, well-respected history which is unique to yerself. Highland, you probably have the most diversity of all of us. Islay, you speak straight and everyone knows what to expect of you. Lowland, you are a bit more refined than the likes of myself and Islay. But you have welcomed all our friends from abroad and without you where would we be? I am more localised than some of you but that is what I do the best.

C – And that's what people want from you, that's what mak's yer character, son.

S – Exactly. So I'll get doon off my high horse and respect all of you here for who you are and all of your differences that make you what you are.

C – Not one of us can represent this country o' oors on our own. We all need each other. We are a' just a part of the Barleycorn family. Without any one of us the family is just no' complete.

I – Aye, we are all as equal as each other here despite size, reputation and popularity. Without any one of us we are incomplete. And what would our business be with an incomplete family? Who would be around to show the foreigners what to do?

*All chuckle*

L – (Standing up) Gentleman, charge your glasses, be upstanding and drink to the family, old and new. To the sons of John Barleycorn.

All – The sons of John Barleycorn. Slainthe.

# Returning

GANNETS

## Kevin Cadwallender

# Homecoming

It's not a question of boundaries,
I don't believe in the arbitrary nature
Of lines drawn by cartographers.

The sun picks out a panel on Tor Ness
Flashes like a paparazzi at my coming home.
Shock of recognition, my adopted land.

Over Traprain Law clouds clamber
The first evidence that home isn't far,
Further on and further into the day
Islands and seats, the dormant volcano.

I pull in to Easter Road, the police
Listen to sectarian songs from both sides.

It's not a question of sides,
My dialect as different to London
As Scots to English.

Somewhere in all of this is a theft.
The Northumbrian inside me reclaiming
The land where the kingdom stood.

At night, a lone woman tightly squeezed
Into an inappropriate high street dress
Belts out an aria from the long gone charts.

But it's not over. I know that.
It's not a question of landscapes

I lie back and think of Scotland.

## Rosie Alexander

### Home

My father's father brought up by an ayah
spoke Hindustani to himself playing in the dust of the yard.
On Sundays he practised his best Scottish accent
And put it on with his smart clothes for his parents inside.

Over the years, he worked on the old chameleon trick
In Edinburgh, where the castle shone behind a coat of black,
In the hospital ships where they patched the damaged men
In Newfoundland where houses and lives slipped over the ice.

And like every generation since, born outside and not within
I feel myself tread the patterns of the kink in a gene
As if we each in our turn perfect the ability to blend,
to let the colours run – like orphaned birds,
over several generations, will find their own song.

## Going South

Like those birds that run into the tide
and out again
I dipped South on the plane
to paddle in the waters of an England
I don't know, a family who are now grown

And caught in the swash of voices
alcohol, noise and gush of too-happy happiness
I felt I could drown – but felt it too late
– it was a close escape.

Now I'm back to a land that isn't mine
I shake my feathers
to let the Orkney air back in
then let the strands rest one against the other
and begin to feel myself again.

## Pam Beasant

### Visitors…

*(for David Malouf, who dislikes the word 'vibrant')*

…move through Stromness
unaware they are patching holes,
bumping ghosts; they touch
stone, thinking it's clean.

They find vegetables, good
coffee; they keep alive

take away atoms of sky
traces of accent, salt.

Sometimes one comes
with more absorbent
mind and eye.

For you, David
I hope standing stones
brood by Aussie lagoons;
St Magnus's fat red pillars
prop the memory
of dappled tombs.

The autumn light (which is
not vibrant – never that)
was a little richer with you here;
is more various for you having
taken it home.

## Sarah Harper

# What Nature Hides

You can hear birds sing
You can hear bells ring
You can hear crunching leaves as you walk

You can smell fresh cold air
You can smell dew from the previous night
You can smell wild flowers

You can see colossal trees
You can see birds flying before you
You can see birds and other creatures

You can eat rolls that have been packed in your lunchbox
You can eat berries and cherries of trees
You can eat fruits of trees

You can touch the rough bark on the trees
You can touch the wax-like leaves
You can touch nature

# Lucy Gibbon

## Help us Find Gingy! A story for children

Pete loves all his pets. Being the son of a farmer, he has plenty to choose from. But his favourite pet is Gingy, an old ginger tom cat, who has been around for as long as Pete can remember. Gingy's only fault is that sometimes, he wanders off for days on end. "Searching the parish for females," Pete's dad would say. But there is one spring when Gingy disappears for longer than usual and everyone begins to get worried.

Finally Pete decides to make up posters to put on notice boards around the village in the hope that someone has seen him. The poster shows a photograph with the plea underneath, "Help Us Find Gingy!" Jim the dairyman's son comes in just as Pete is finishing his posters and picks one up. "You know," he says, "I'm sure I saw a ginger cat this morning as I helped my dad take the cows down the road. It was running into the wood, chasing rabbits. Maybe you should try looking there."

"I am not going into that wood by myself," says Pete, "It's haunted!"

"Don't be silly," says his dad, "you've been listening to the stories the old men of the village tell, they're just foolin' you."

Now Pete, who is usually quite a confident lad of nine, is still a bit afraid of going into the wood alone, despite what his dad says. The wood itself is an interesting and intriguing place, but parts of it are very dark and mysterious.

"Never mind," says Jim, "I'll come with you. We can look around this afternoon."

After searching the wood for what seems like hours, Pete and Jim are both on the verge of giving up, when they see a flash of ginger sweep past them. They both follow in the same direction along a long narrow path they had not noticed before. The long winding path eventually opens up into a clearing. In the centre of the clearing is an old stone cottage. They can see smoke rising from the chimney and the front door is ajar. Again they both think they see a ginger tail disappear around the door of the cottage.

They walk up to the building and Jim knocks on the front door. There is no answer, so he knocks again, still no answer. "There's no-one home" says Pete, "Let's go inside, I'm sure I saw Gingy go in." Before Jim can stop him, Pete pushes the door open wider and enters the cottage. Jim has no choice but to follow him.

While Pete and Jim are looking around the cottage, calling for Gingy, they are unaware that an old man is standing on the threshold of the door watching them. He is dressed with a piece of baler twine tied round his waist to hold up his trousers. He is also wearing big boots, a great overcoat, and a woolly hat, and sports a stubbly beard. He is carrying two dead rabbits.

"What you doing in my house?" he shouts with a thick local accent. Pete and Jim both jump with fright. They have been caught snooping around someone's home! They turn round to face the stranger.

Pete and Jim both start murmuring apologies together, too startled to think straight. The strange man puts up his gnarled old hand and says, "Now, now there'll be none of that garblin', one of you at a time – you boy!" He points directly at Pete."You look like an honest sort o' kid, tell me what you're up to!" Pete looks at Jim, takes a deep breath, and proceeds to explain to the old man about Gingy and how upset they all are at losing him and that they thought they had seen him go through the cottage door.

The old man's attitude seems to soften during the explanation and after Pete finishes he actually smiles and says, "Well it's grand in this day an' age that a pet is so well cared for and loved." Then the old man strides past them towards the fireplace, dumps the dead rabbits on the table and says, "I'd very much like it if you'd stay and share some of my food."

Pete and Jim are still feeling a bit guilty, so they decide it would be okay to stay to tea. Before long they are all enjoying some rabbit stew sitting round a roaring fire. They all have a great time talking about what it is like growing up around the wood and about all the adventures they have had. Pete feels strangely comfortable around the old man, as if he has known him a long time. At one point the old man produces a fiddle and begins playing a wild sweet dancing tune. Pete and Jim can't resist getting up and stomping around the room.

When the music dies down, Jim looks out of the window and realises it is getting dark outside. "Oh Lord" he says, "I'd better be getting you home, Pete, we've stayed in the wood far too long". The old man seems quite upset that they were leaving, but he does not stop them, "Ta now, thanks for stoppin' by and... I'm sure you will find your cat soon" he says while winking at Pete. Pete is puzzled by this gesture but waves goodbye to the old man and follows Jim out of the wood and back up the farm road.

Pete's dad is very angry that they get back so late, but he is intrigued by the mention of the old man in the cottage. "I didn't know there were any cottages in the wood that were fit to live in. I'd like to see it for myself and meet this new friend of yours".

So the next morning all three of them head back into the wood. But when they get to the clearing, there is no cottage, only the remains of an old chimney and bit of a wall where there obviously used to be a cottage. The old man is nowhere in sight either. Pete and Jim look in amazement at each other, they cannot understand it - how can a cottage become a ruin in one night! Just then, a movement from the old chimney stack makes them all look round. A cat jumps up onto the wall and begins licking its paws.

It's Gingy!

CORMORANTS

# Biographies

**Rosie Alexander** juggles writing poetry with her work as a counsellor and careers adviser. She has a particular interest in the use of creative writing for self-discovery.

**Amy Allan**: I'm alright. A little neurotic, perhaps; a bit sore. But I've loved them, and that matters to me. My name's Amy, and I'd like to write more.

**Pam Beasant** lives in Stromness and writes poetry, prose and non-fiction. She was the first GMB Fellow in 2007.

**Kate Barrett**'s poetry was first published when she was 12 years old. She has never stopped writing, having worked in theatre, television, publishing and publicity. Her poem, "Red Head" was written while her latest husband was dying of cancer.

**Kevin Cadwallender** performs poetry in the unusual places, supermarkets, buses and golf tournaments included. Books 'Sagrada Familia' (RSP) and 'Dances with Vowels' (Smokestack) and is commissioning editor for Red Squirrel Press Scotland.

**Amber Connolly** still remembers the joy of writing her first lengthy poem about deserts in primary school – except it wasn't, as her teacher smilingly pointed out – it was about desserts! Undeterred, she continues to try.

**Bill Ferguson** has spent a lifetime flouting the laws of gravity. One day they will have their revenge.

**Ron Ferguson** is an award-winning journalist and the author of 14 books. His biography of George MacLeod was shortlisted for the Scottish Writer of the Year Award.

**Alison Flett** was born and bred in Edinburgh but has lived in Orkney for more than 10 years. Her collection of poetry *Whit Lassyz Ur Inty* was published by Argyll Press in 2004. She has recently moved to Australia.

**Fran Flett Hollinrake** is a writer, historian and storyteller and lives in Quoyloo. She is currently writing a book full of stories about the dark side of Orkney history.

**Lucy Gibbon**, of the Stromness Writing Group, began writing children's stories to entertain her nephews. She draws inspiration from them and from her memories of growing up on a farm in Dumfriesshire.

**Yvonne Gray** is a writer and musician. She is married with three sons. Her first poetry collection, *In the Hanging Valley*, was published by Two Ravens Press in 2008.

**Mandy Haggith** writes from a woodland croft in Assynt in the Northwest Highlands. She founded the community arts company, Top Left Corner, which runs the "best writing retreat in Western Europe".

**Sarah Harper**, aged nine, likes kayaking, swimming, rock-climbing, craft-work, computer design, gardening, cooking and baking. She hopes to work with dolphins in California or Florida one day.

**Lesley Harrison** lives on Eday. Her poem, "Red Head" is the beginning of a sequence of poems about the island. Red Head is Eday's most northerly point.

Like fishermen who farm, **Sylvia Hays** is a painter who writes. Orkney has been her home for more than twenty years.

**Mike Hoy** and his family moved to Orkney two years ago. This is his second writing venture – his first being his wedding vows. He helps run the Orkney Whisky Club in his spare time.

**Carola Huttmann** draws much of her creative inspiration from the richness of tradition, history and tranquil charm of the Orkney Islands, her home since 1995.

**Lynn Johnson** is originally from Staffordshire and took up creative writing when she moved to Orkney five years ago. Since then she has written short stories and is working on her first novel.

**David Lea** worked mainly with birds from 1950 when he became Warden on Lundy Island. He was RSPB Orkney Officer from 1973, then ran Go-Orkney Tours for 13 years from 1982.

**Anna Lipinska** was born and brought up in Yorkshire. Self confessed dilettante, trained nurse and Further Education lecturer, she has seen service with the Royal Air Force and civilian police. Recently awarded PhD Criminal Justice.

**LC Littlejohn** is a columnist for *Orkney Today* and regularly writes articles for magazines. Presently she is working on a romantic novel.

**Ragnhild Ljosland** is originally from Norway, but moved to Kirkwall with her Orcadian husband and children in 2009. She works for the Centre for Nordic Studies, Orkney College. Orcadian at heart.

**Morag MacInnes** was born and bred in Orkney and returned seven years ago to find it much changed in many ways and also much the same.

Originally from Oban, **Kirsty Macdonald** lives in Kirkwall and teaches literature at Orkney College UHI. She writes poetry and prose, and is currently working on a science fiction novel.

**John McGill** lives in Quoyloo.

**Nalini Paul** is the George Mackay Brown Writing Fellow (2009-10) and currently lives in Stromness. She was born in India and grew up in Canada. Her poetry chap book, *Skirlags*, was shortlisted for this year's Callum Macdonald Memorial Award.

**Alistair Peebles** has lived and worked in Orkney since 1985. He was educated in Glasgow and Aberdeen. He is currently researching Ian Hamilton Finlay's visits to Rousay in the 1950s.

**Tessa Ransford** is a poet, translator, literary editor and cultural activist. Founder and former director of the Scottish Poetry Library, she initiated the annual Callum Macdonald Memorial Award for publishers of pamphlet poetry in Scotland. Tessa's *Not Just Moonshine, New and Selected Poems* was published by Luath Press (2008).

**Doreen Sinclair:** I am retired and enjoy writing when in the mood. I prefer to write poetry and short stories being too lazy to attempt a novel.

Since retiring from teaching and working for examination boards, **Margaret Storr** has spent time painting, gardening and singing in the Festival Choir. And writing!

**Catherine Turnbull** is editor of *Orkney Today* newspaper. She has won an award for play-writing, been shortlisted for poetry and short story awards, and is writing her first novel.

**Christie Williamson** is a poet from Yell, Shetland. His debut pamphlet, *Arc o Möns*, translations of Lorca's poetry into Shetland, was joint winner of the 2010 Callum Macdonald Memorial Award.